I0689382

Betrayal & Deceit
To take over the mean streets of Philly
by Author: Jerz Toston

Betrayal & Deceit

By: Jerz Toston

Cover Designed By: LeRoy Grayson–Choice Media Studios

Cover Picture Female Model: Chan'tel Henry

Logo Designs By: Andre M. Saunders

Editor: Anelda L. Attaway

ACKNOWLEDGMENTS

First and Foremost, I'd like to give thanks and all praise to Allah (SWT) without Him none of this would be possible. I want to let my kids know that this is for yall; Sikai, Meesh, Lil Jerz, DeIvyan, Riya, and Jah'ceer. Daddy luv yall.

Also I want to tell my better half my wife Tambra, I luv you until tha death of me and thanks for putting up wit my shit when you didn't have to. Luv you babe.

Also my mom, I told you I'd make you proud of me. This is only tha beginning.

My sisters Ericka, Felisha, and my other sis Nika and my bro Lbs. Def can't forget about my folks on Bang Bang Killer, Chulo, Hov, Shaffee, Rupt and Big Head and tha rest...this is where it all started. Luv you Niggaz.

RIP to all my folks that left us to soon...to many names but know that ya G.B.N.F.

All my folks behind those walls. Matim told you I was gone to do it, FREE C. How I got yall until they FREE yall.

DEDICATIONS

This book is dedicated to Mom Betty and Moe Good. I know yall are smiling down on me.

I Luv yall

TABLE OF CONTENTS

INTRODUCTION i

CHAPTER 1 - Zoey and Zell Cousins, Go to tha Club 01

CHAPTER 2 - Zoey is Notified about Quez's Death 08

CHAPTER 3 - Quez's Funeral 11

CHAPTER 4 - The Shipment Quez Left Needs to Move 13

CHAPTER 5 - Zoey Takes Over tha Game for Quez 17

CHAPTER 6 - Cal Need Some Work 25

CHAPTER 7 - Joey's Cousin Parker Dealt Wit 28

CHAPTER 8 - Some Good Weed…Cheap! 31

CHAPTER 9 - Happy 4th Birthday Calry 33

CHAPTER 10 - Zoacis Styles & Cutz 37

CHAPTER 11 - Pit Tried to Set Me Up 39

CHAPTER 12 - The Rat Pit is Poisoned, Tortured and Killed 43

CHAPTER 13 - LT and Rosco Plotting to Take tha City Over 47

CHAPTER 14 - At Ms. Tootsies Discussing Biz-ness? 48

CHAPTER 15 - BLING…Ciara's Ring 51

CHAPTER 16 - Zoey Finds Out that Quez was Murdered 53

CHAPTER 17 - Zoacis Styles & Cutz Grand Opening 55

CHAPTER 18 - Tha Auction 61

CHAPTER 19 - Handlin Biz-ness 64

TABLE OF CONTENTS

CHAPTER 20 - Ms. Wilma's House and Tha Bet............67

CHAPTER 21 - Spence asked Zoey to Marry Him............75

CHAPTER 22 - Cookin tha Work and Watchin tha Block 79

CHAPTER 23 - Zoey and Tweek Become Friends 88

CHAPTER 24 - Tha Plan............96

CHAPTER 25 - Planning an End to Zoey's Reign............98

CHAPTER 26 - Tweek and Zoey Goes Out 101

CHAPTER 27 - Tweek and Zoey Coincidentally Meet............112

CHAPTER 28 - Box Works tha Block............114

CHAPTER 29 - Where is tha Money and tha Drugs? 121

CHAPTER 30 - Tweek and Zoey Spends Quality Time............125

CHAPTER 31 - Tha Hit at Ms. Wilma's House 132

CHAPTER 32 - Draft Day............140

CHAPTER 33 - Taking it to tha Next Level............143

CHAPTER 34 - Everybody Down! 167

CHAPTER 35 - Jibbs Lies to Zoey and tha Betrayal Starts 175

CHAPTER 36 - Jibbs Try'n to Sell tha Work for More............187

CHAPTER 37 - Ciara is Going to be Surprised 191

CHAPTER 38 - Stick ups Instead of Hustling............201

CHAPTER 39 - The Vacation in tha Dominican 211

TABLE OF CONTENTS

CHAPTER 40 - No Loyalty, No Remorse 219

CHAPTER 41 - Revenge, Rosco, LT, and Bo Get Killed 225

CHAPTER 42 - Ms. Wilma Reveals Disturbing News 229

CHAPTER 43 - Kill 3 Birds wit One Stone 232

CHAPTER 44 - Betray and Deceit a Deadly Combination 236

ABOUT THE AUTHOR 241

INTRODUCTION

Zoey was left no choice but to take over tha mean streets of Philly when her fiancé Quez was murdered. She vowed to bring tha killer to street justice wit tha help of her cousins, Jibbs and Zell along wit her nephews' father Cal. But everything ain't always what it seems.

On her rise to tha top; who can she trust? They say keep ya friends & enemies close, but family even closer.

So take this real ride wit us through tha murderous and drug infested streets of Philly on a journey of Betrayal & Deceit.

CHAPTER 1

Zoey and Zell Cousins, Go to tha Club

"I'm so sick of his shit."

"Girl I don't know why you even put up wit it, if it was me he would've been kicked to tha curb."

"I know, but Zell you know I love him to death."

"Zoey love is like a drug; once you get hooked you have to find tha strength to get unhooked!"

"Easier said than done, I've been hooked for ten years."

"So what did Quez do now?"

"Mya called me and said she saw some Bitch driving his car yesterday."

"Girl, you still listening to hatin' ass Mya?"

"Why would she lie about something like that?"

"I know that's ya cousin, but I still think she wants him."

"She's ya cousin too."

"Please don't remind me."

"Ha! Ha! Ha! Zell you stupid as shit."

"Whaaat ever, you better watch her."

"I wish she would, I'll Fuck both of them up."

"Are you going to tha club tonight?"

"I was thinking about it."

"Or should I say is Quez gonna let you go to tha club tonight?"

"Bitch please, he don't control shit!"

"That's what ya mouth say."

"Well, you just make sure you come back to pick me up."

"Oh I'll be back, you just make sure ya slow ass is ready."

"What time you comin back?"

"It's 8 o'clock now, so I'll be back no later than 10 o'clock."

"A'ight, I'll be ready."

"You better or you'll be left."

"What ever, bye Hussy."

Zell was my cousin, but we were tight like sisters, people even say we look alike. 5'7", hazel eyes, shoulder length hair, caramel complexion and an ass that would make tha rapper Trina mad. Zell was tha same except she had a short haircut and smaller booty.

After, I got out tha shower I walked in my closet to find me tha perfect outfit. After about 15 minutes, I decided on my brown Gucci dress wit tha matching sandals. By tha time I was dressed, Zell was out front beeping tha horn.

"Bitch if you don't stop honking that mafuckin horn!"

"Well, come on then."

"Bout time you washed this car."

"Bitch like you need to talk."

"My car stays clean."

"Yeah only cause Quez keeps it clean."

"So what."

"Zoey I was thinking about trading this in and get me tha new Caddy Wagon."

"Wow, those are real nice."

"I'll be glad when Spence go to tha league."

"I thought he was coming out last year?"

"He decided to wait until this year so he can go top 5."

"Everybody said he'll probably go top 2."

"Well, all I know is a Bitch was wit him from day one."

"I know that's right."

"He better put a ring on this finger," she said holding her hand up.

"I know he gonna be knocking broads off so if I got tha ring it won't matter to me."

"Not to mention tha pay day you'll get if you divorce him."

"Divorce? Girl yeah right. Imma get all that I can, and then I'll file," she said slapping me five.

"You just make sure you put a lot of doe in tha bank."

"You already know I am."

"Damn, it ain't never no parking spots close."

"Pull into that parking lot right there."

"I'm not paying 20 dollars to park."

"Just pull in there, I'll pay tha fee."

We paid and walked to tha club where tha line was long as hell.

"This line is too long."

"That's because Jeezy is performing tonight," some guy said.

Zell why didn't you tell me Jeezy was performing, I would have got sharp?"

"I didn't even know, you see how I look."

"Damn I would love to see yall all dressed up then," tha same guy said.

"Zoey, Zell..." We both looked to see who was callin our names.

"Up here come on!" When we got to tha front of tha line our cousin

Jibbs and his boys were up there.

"I know yall wasn't going to wait in that long ass line?"

"No, I was about to tell Zell that we were about to go VIP."

"Did Quez get back in town yet?"

"No he'll be back in tha morning."

We got inside and Jibbs told us to put our money up, he had us covered. It was so packed inside there was no way all of those people outside was going to get in here tonight.

"Yall good? We bout to do a little mingling."

"Yeah thanks Cuz."

"No need to thank me, we peeps."

"Come on Zoey let's get a drink."

"I'm right behind you."

"What you drinking?"

"Long Island Ice Tea?" After waiting 10 minutes tha bartender finally took our order.

"Next time get yall drinks from VIP, it'll be much faster."

As I took my drink I said, "Thanks for tha advice."

"Any time," he responded wit a wink.

"Looks like he likes you."

"Sorry already taken."

"Hey cousins, why yall didn't call me to come out wit yall?" I knew Zell was about to say something smart so I said, "You told me you wasn't going out no more."

"Did I? That must have been tha next day when I woke up all hung over."

"From what I hear, you always drunk in tha club."

"Not tonight, my brother is in here."

"I know, he got us in past all those people out there."

"He's so full of it, when I called him he told me he wasn't coming."

"I wonder why?"

"Zell I'm not for ya shit tonight."

"Fine, come on Zoey let's see what's going on in tha VIP."

"Oh yall in VIP too?" she asked showing her VIP bracelet.

"I'll meet yall in there, I gotta get my girls."

"I wonder whose dick she sucked to get that."

"Zell you ain't right, she's still family."

"Please don't remind me."

All tha ballers were in VIP and they made it no secret they had money to play wit, it was chump change compared to what Quez was holding. 9 outta 10 they were all either copping from him or hustling his work.

"Damn Zell, you lookin' real good tonight."

"Thank you."

"You still wit that nigga Spence?"

"Yup."

"Word is he's going to tha league in a few months when tha draft comes."

"I don't know, I don't keep up wit that stuff."

"Tell that to somebody who might believe it."

"What ever Roc."

"Can I buy you and ya peeps a drink?"

"Yes you can," Mya said not letting Zell respond. Zell looked at her like she was crazy.

"What yall drinkin Long Islands?"

"Yeah."

"Not me, I'll take some Remy."

"Oh you a big girl huh?"

"Look at her, all in his face."

"You know how she gets down so it shouldn't even surprise you."

"She just makes me mad wit that shit, it ain't like she's ugly."

"I'm bout to get my party on, she's not going to ruin my night."

"Mine either, come on."

Tha song came on…*I JUST WANT THA MONEY, MONEY AND THA CARS, CARS AND THA CLOTHES; I SUPPOSE I JUST WANT TO BE SUCCESSFUL.*"

"This my shit right here."

"Yall a'ight?"

"Yeah we good Cuz."

"Jibbs ya sister in VIP."

"Is she drunk yet?"

"No."

"Man I swear I don't feel like babysitting, I'm try'n to enjoy myself tonight:"

"Yall wanna take a couple flicks, I gotta send my man some flicks."

"When do Rizzo get out?"

"Next year."

"It seems like he's been locked up forever."

"He had 7 mandy."

"I know he's ready to come home."

Next, we ended up taking over 15 pictures. Of course me and Zell had to get some together and solo.

Jeezy hit tha stage in tha whole club went crazy. He performed some of his classic hits like Trap Star, My Hood and Put On. When he was done he went to tha VIP lounge. All tha groupies, males and females were try'n to get in, but unless they had a wristband they were denied.

"You need a band to get in here." We just held up our wrist and were let in.

"Umm, Umm, Umm look at her," Zell said referring to Mya. I walked over to Mya and yanked her by tha arm.

"You need to chill out!"

"Zoey get off me," she said pulling her arm away.

Jibbs walked in as she was pulling away, so not to cause a scene he said, "Mya let me holla at you." He pulled her to tha side and said a few words then went to tha bar.

"Thank you Cuz."

"Zoey I should be thanking you; now you see what I mean about babysitting."

"I thought I was in a strip club when I walked in here."

"Ha! Ha! Ha! Zell you crazy."

"Nah Cuz seriously, she was giving a lap dance."

"What ever you said made her calm down.

"I just told her if she didn't calm down, I was gonna kick her ass right here. I wish she was more like you two." We partied for tha rest of tha night in VIP. We even got to take a few pictures wit Jeezy.

CHAPTER 2

Zoey is Notified about Quez's Death

By tha time I got home I was tired as shit. I heated up some spaghetti then headed upstairs. After I ate I took a nice hot bath then went to bed. Tha phone kept ringing non-stop so I finally answered it.

"Hello?" I answered wit much attitude.

"Is this Ms. Brown?"

"Yes it is and who is this calling my house at 5 in tha morning?"

"Ms. Brown this is Detective Shaw, if you could please be so kind come down to tha station." *Oh my God! Instantly I thought about Quez, I hope he didn't get busted coming back.*

"Why do you need me to come down to tha station?"

"This isn't something I would want to discuss over tha phone."

"Is my fiancé a'ight?"

"Like I just stated, this isn't something to discuss over tha phone."

"OK, I'm on my way down there now."

20 minutes later I was walking into tha police station nervous about what I was about to hear.

"Yes, I'm here to see Detective Shaw." She pointed to a guy in a black designer suit. *"He looks more like a hustler than a cop," I thought to myself.*

"Hello Ms. Brown I'm Detective Shaw, follow me please." He took me to one of those interviewing rooms. *"What tha hell has Quez gotten me into?"*

"Ms. Brown, this is tha part of my job I hate tha most; there's no easy way to say this so Imma just say it. Ya fiancé was killed by a drunk driver." My mouth dropped open while I was try'n to register what I thought he just said.

When I didn't respond Detective Shaw said, "Ms. Brown did you hear me? Ya fiancé was killed by a drunk driver this morning."

"Nooooooo! Nooooooooo! He is not dead! Don't you say that!"

"Ms. Brown I'm going to need you to go down to tha morgue wit me and identify tha body."

As soon as we got there tha Medical Examiner pulled tha sheet back and I lost it.

"Noooooo not my Baaaaaby! Nooooooo God Whyyyyyy!"

"Ms. Brown is there someone I could call for you?"

Tha last thing I remember was giving him Zell's name and number, and then everything went black. When I came to, I saw Zell and my moms face.

"Zell I had tha craziest dream ever, I dreamt that this detective called me and told me to come to tha station. When I got there he told me Quez had been killed, and then he had me look at his body. Girl that dream felt so real."

"Baby that was no dream," my mom said wit tears in her eyes. I looked at Zell who too had tears in her eyes.

"No! No! No! No! My Baby is not dead! He can't be I just talked to him. Mommy please tell me he's not dead pleeeeeease!"

"Baby I'm sorry, but Quez is gone."

"Noooooo! Aaaaaaaagghh!" After about an hour Zoey fell asleep.

"Aunt Zeida, I'm going to stay wit her until she gets over this."

"Gizelle that could be a very long time."

"I know, but she's gonna need family around her right now, especially getting everything right for his funeral."

"Thank you."

"Aunty you don't have to thank me."

CHAPTER 3

Quez's Funeral

It was tha day of tha funeral and I didn't want to get outta bed.

"Come on Zoey, get up and get ready; Quez's father will be here in an hour." My eyes were so red from lack of sleep and crying.

After I got out of tha shower, Zell had my clothes laid out on tha bed for me. I put tha dress and shoes back in tha closet.

"Zoey come on it's time to go!" Zell yelled up tha steps.

I sprayed some Wish 'Kimora Lee Simmon' Perfume on, grabbed my Gucci shades and headed downstairs.

"Why did you put that dress on?"

"Because everybody else is going to be wearing black. I'm wearing white because I'm not mourning his death, I'm celebrating his life into Heaven." Zell gave me a big hug.

When tha Limo pulled up I knew it was Mr. Santiago, Quez's father. Quez's father was Dominican and his mother was Black.

"Hello Zoey, sorry we had to see each other under these conditions."

"So am I."

"Did you have enough money to cover tha funeral expenses?"

"Yes."

"Once tha funeral is over there are few things I need to talk to you about."

When we pulled up to tha church, it looked more like a concert and a car show than a funeral.

"My son knew all these people?"

"Mr. Santiago ya son ran this town which I'm sure you already know."

"Zoey I always thought my son would lose his life to tha streets if he died, not to some drunk old man. It's funny how things happen. I never wanted my son to follow in my footsteps, but since he did, I had no choice but to be his supplier."

"Mr. Santiago, Quez always spoke highly of you."

"Zoey I blamed myself for his mother dying, but Quez helped me to get through it." Mr. Santiago broke down right there in tha Limo.

After a few minutes he wiped his tears and said, "Now that I've got that out, let's go send my son to Heaven to watch over us."

We walked into tha church and all eyes were on us as we were shown to tha front row. I could hear people whispering about how much Quez and his dad looks alike. There were so many people wit T-Shirts wit Quez on them that said, "KING OF PHILLY GONE BUT NEVER FORGOTTEN."

I tried to hold it together, but I just couldn't. So when it was my turn to speak, I couldn't do it. But since I had it written down Zell got up to speak for me. I cried out and cried out, and cried out. I could not believe my Quez was gone forever.

At tha final viewing, a lot of people put money in tha casket. I stood over top of my Baby to see his face for tha last time. "Nooooooo God! Whyyyyyy you take my Baaaaby!" Mr. Santiago and Zell had to pull me away from tha casket, but I wasn't ready to say goodbye to Quez forever.

CHAPTER 4

The Shipment Quez Left Needs to Move

After we left tha burial we went to tha hall that I rented for tha repass.

"I'm so tired of everybody being fake."

"What are you talking about?"

"All these mafuckas just try'n to take my Baby spot."

"Since you mentioned it, that's one of tha things I need to talk to you about. Quez just paid me for a shipment and if you want it, it's yours." *"I could just give it to my cousin Jibbs to sell for me," I thought to myself.*

"Sure, I'll get rid of it."

"Quez told me he schooled you on tha game in case anything was to happen to him and you had to take over."

"Yeah he did."

"Well after you're done wit this, if you wish to continue you have my support.

"Quez also told me to give you this," he said handing me a key.

"This is to a safety-deposit box; he said you'll know where it is."

Mr. Santiago made a call then said that tha shipment would be delivered to tha storage room, which I knew where it was from going wit Quez a few times.

"Well I need to get back down tha highway. You have my number, call me if you run into any problems…any."

"So are you really going to sell that stuff?"

"Yeah, I'll let Jibbs do it; it's probably only a few bricks; that should not be a problem."

I left tha hall and headed straight to tha safety-deposit box. When I got there I was a little hesitant to open it, afraid of what might be inside. When I did, there was an envelope wit my name on it. I opened it to find a note and another key.

My beautiful Zoey,

If you're reading this then 1 of 3 things have happened; I'm locked up, I'm dead, or we have broken it off. If I'm lucky, you just somehow found tha key and chose to be nosey. LOL But if that is not tha case take this key and tha contents that are inside of this box, it should hold you down and that's not including all tha money you been stashing for tha past 10 years. LOL Yes I know about it and that's why I love you so much. Zoey, just always remember and know I love you until I'm dead and gone, and I'll still love you from Heaven.

Love Quez

I couldn't hold back my tears after reading that letter, but I had to be strong for Quez. When I opened up tha other box I couldn't believe my eyes. There had to be at least a couple hundred thousand in there, but what stood out tha most was tha diamond necklace wit tha diamond heart that had our picture in it. I wasted no time putting it on. I decided to leave tha money inside, then headed to tha storage place.

"Holy Shit! Wow this is way more than I expected it to be. How can I get rid of all this work?" It turned out to be 55 bricks. I called Mr. Santiago to find out how much he was charging Quez. When it was all said and done I would charge 28,000 instead of tha 30,000. As I was on my way home, Jibbs called me.

"Hey Cuz, just checking up on you. Are you OK?"

"Yeah, where are you at?"

"I'm in tha hood like roaches."

"Stay there I'm on my way, I need to holla at you."

"I ain't going nowhere, I'll be here."

30 minutes later I was pulling up on 19th & Masters.

"What up Cuz?"

"Look, Imma get straight to tha point, since Quez is gone, who's tha city gonna cop off?"

"Funny you asked that, a lot of people have been calling me to see if you had some of his work."

"Well, let them know I got them for 28,000 and I already know Quez was them letting go for 30,000; so don't try no slick shit cause I'm not having it."

"Jibbs how much was you grabbing?"

"Cuz, I was only doing a half a jawn."

"I thought you was grabbing heavy tha way this block do numbers."

"Yeah, I was gonna start grabbing a whole pie."

"Well look, I'm going to give you 5 bricks at 30,000 a piece since I'm hitting you on consignment. Are you cool wit that?"

"Hell yeah! I'm cool wit that."

"Only thing, I don't want you selling no weight, break 'em down; sell all dimes, halfs and bundles. What else do yall move on this block?"

"Weed, pills and a little syrup."

"Give me about a month and I'll have all tha weed, syrup and pills you'll need."

"Damn Cuz, listen to you; if I didn't know any better, I would've thought you been in this game for years."

"I have, I just never sold nothing."

"I feel you, Quez has taught you well. When you gonna bring tha work back?"

"Back? I have it right now."

"Well drive me around tha corner to my Stash House."

"Jibbs you don't have to rush, but don't take 3 months either."

"Ha! Ha! Ha! Cuz you funny as hell, I should be calling you in 5 days or less."

"A'ight just be safe and in tha mean time you can tell them to call Quez's hitter."

I pulled off and headed home to get some rest.

CHAPTER 5

Zoey Takes Over tha Game

"Zoey you sure you know what you're getting into?"

"Zell, I don't have a choice, I can't let somebody else take what Quez worked so hard to build."

"Why do you care who takes over? You're set for life."

"It's tha principle. Either you got my back or you don't!"

"That goes wit out saying, but you know there's no turning back once we're in."

"Zell I'm already in!"

"Well, so am I then."

"Come on, we have a meeting to go to."

"What kind of meeting is this?"

"Why?"

"I need to know if I need to bring this," she said pulling her Cat 9 outta her Coach bag.

"Bitch when you get a gun?"

"I had this for a while and yes it is legal. I just got my license to carry too. In this line of work you never know when you might have to handle biz-ness."

When we pulled up to tha Warehouse, there were about 15 cars there.

"What up Cuz? Is everybody here?"

"Everybody except him," he said pointing to Joey who was just pulling up wit his music all tha way up.

I didn't say shit. I just walked in to get tha show on tha road.

"I know you're all wondering why you're here, tha reason for this meeting is to establish a few things. As you all know Quez was killed 2 weeks ago and he supplied all of you wit drugs. Correct?" Everybody shook their heads in agreement. "If there is anybody who doesn't want to do biz-ness wit me speak up now."

Nobody said anything at first, and then Joey spoke up, "You do know that Quez was only charging us 22,500." Tha whole room looked at Joey but said nothing.

"No...but what I do know is that I'm charging you 28,000 which is about 2,000 less than you were paying. You see Joey, I don't like a liar or a get over. And tha next time you come to a meeting, do not pull up wit that music loud like that again. Are we clear?"

"I paid for that system so I'll play it as loud as I want. I don't work for you, you need my money."

He was try'n to play me in front of everybody and if I let him get away wit it, tha rest of them would consider me as weak. So I needed to set tha record straight right now.

I pulled out my 40 Cal, "You see Joey that's where you're wrong. I don't need ya money, hell I don't even need you."

"Bitch wit out me or us you can't get rid of ya drugs."

"I don't need you and just to show you...BANG! BANG! BANG! BANG! BANG! BANG! I kept shooting until tha whole clip was empty.

"Now that we got that settled back to biz-ness." I looked at everybody's face so they could see tha seriousness in mine. Tha funny thing is I could see and sense tha fear in them now. "I know that Quez was charging 30,000, so for me to let them go at 28,000 is a steal. Is everyone a'ight wit that?" They all nodded.

"Would anyone have a problem wit me fronting them some extra bricks?"

"Hell naw, not me; me either," some responded wit.

"OK, let's see how this first shipment goes. If nobody has any other questions or concerns this is over."

"Thank you Zoey."

"For what AZ?" he asked as he pointed to Joey.

"I was about to push his shit back because he was try'n to move in on my block."

Jibbs put him in his car, drove to an isolated spot and set him and his car on fire.

When we left Zell said, "Bitch you crazy."

"Looks can be deceiving," was all I responded wit.

"Well one thing for sure and two things for certain, if they didn't respect or fear you before, they definitely do now."

"That's good cause like Quez always said, respect and fear goes along way."

"Let's go to Ms. Tootsies, I'm starving."

"Sounds good, I'm hungry too."

"Hello ladies, dining in or taking out?"

"In."

"Follow me please…would you like something to drink while you look over tha menu?"

"Yes, I'll have some homemade ice tea."

"And I'll have tha lemonade please."

"OK, coming right up."

"I already know what I want; tha fried fish wit macaroni and cheese and fried cabbage."

"I'm going wit tha fried breast, macaroni and cheese, collard greens, and a side of fried shrimp."

When tha waitress came back we repeated our orders. I started thinking about Quez and before I knew it, tears were coming down my eyes.

"You miss him don't you?"

"A whole lot, I try to stay busy so I don't have to think about him, but I can't stop missing him."

"That's how I feel about Spence and he's only in college, so I know how you must feel."

After we finished eating we went to tha tattoo shop.

"May I help you?"

"Yes, I want to get a portrait done."

"Do you have tha picture?"

"Yes," I said handing it to him.

"Wow."

"What's wrong?"

"Nothing this picture is perfect, I'm gonna need an hour to draw it up."

"How long will it take you to do it?"

"How big and where do you want it?" I pulled up my sleeve to show him.

"That'll take me at least 2½ hours."

"Fine."

"It's also gonna cost $350.00."

"I don't care how much it cost as long as it's detailed."

"I'm tha best tattooist in Philly."

"Since it's going to take you an hour to draw it up, I'm going down tha street to Unica."

"Just make sure you come back in an hour."

"I'm about to get a tattoo so go ahead."

"What are you about to get?"

"My Baby's name."

"OK, I'll be back."

I grabbed my nephew an outfit for his birthday, which is in 3 days, then went back to tha shop.

"I was a just about to call you."

"For what?"

"He was done."

"He said one hour. It's only been 45 minutes."

"That's why I was going to call you."

He showed me tha picture and it was perfect. 2 hours later he was done and when I looked at it I broke down.

"What's wrong…you don't like it?"

"No I love it, it looks exactly like him."

"You have to excuse her, he was just killed two weeks ago."

"Oh I'm sorry to hear that."

"Ya work is beautiful. Do you have a card or number where I can reach you so tha next time I can call to make an appointment?"

"Sure…so that means you'll be back?"

"Definitely." He handed me his card that had his cell and shop number.

"If it's after tha shop is closed, I'll come to ya house or if you know anyone that's try'n to have a tattoo party give me a call."

"You know I gotcha Chad."

"You got Calry something?"

"Yeah, you know his birthday is Saturday."

"Oh shit, I totally forgot wit all that's been going on."

"If Ciara didn't call me this morning I would've forgot too."

"Walk me down here so I can grab him something." I ended up buying him two more outfits.

(THE PHONE RINGS: BLOOD THICKER THAN WATER ONLY IN CERTAIN CASES YOU NEED WATER TO LIVE)

"Whats up Jibbs?" I asked answering my phone.

"I took care of ya grass like you asked me to."

"Did you make sure you cleaned everything up when you were done?"

"Yeah you straight."

"A'ight thanks, I'll straighten you out."

"Don't worry about it, as much as you do for me."

"I need to call Mr. Santiago to let him know I'll be needing to place a bigger order."

"You done that 55 already?"

"Just about, I don't want to wait until I'm done."

"Girl, Quez has taught you real well."

(CALLING MR. SANTIAGO)

"Hello Mr. Santiago."

"Ola (Hello)."

"I need to place an order for some chicken."

"ok cuánto (OK, how much?)."

"Cien (100)."

"Wow you're not playing any games."

"I had to move fast because I wasn't going to let anyone take over what Quez started."

Since I knew that we both were on burn outs that we got just to talk to each other on so I decided to tell him about Joey.

"Zoey let me deal wit that part of tha biz-ness."

"Mr. Santiago."

"No, no please no more Mr. Santiago, you are family, call me Javier."

"OK Javier, I respect you, but sometimes things need to be handled right then and there."

"I understand, but if it's something that can wait, you call me and I'll handle it, no need to get ya hands dirty."

"I would really like to handle my own."

"Zoey you're just like Quez in so many ways."

"When do you want me to drive down?"

"Oh no, you don't have to drive, I'll bring it to you, jus have tha money and tha storage spot."

"I'll have tha money there in a few hours."

"Ok but tha product won't be there until noon tomorrow."

As I was hanging up Ciara was calling on my other phone.

"Hello."

"Hey Zoey how you feeling?

"I'm OK, just came from getting Calry a few outfits; me and Zell."

"I need a big, big favor."

"How much do you need?"

"Who said I needed money?"

"Well most of tha time when you need a big favor, it involves money."

"Calry's dad does not have tha money for tha cake and I spent what I had on his party."

"How much do you need?"

"I have to call and see, I think its $150 though."

"Damn, what you get a talkin cake?"

"No, but I did get his face on it."

"Well, find out how much it is and call me back." Call Disconnected.

"Zell I swear Calry's dad ain't worth shit."

"Well I thought he hustled?"

"If he do, I can't tell, he's always broke."

"Why don't you hit him wit some work?"

"Because I don't want him or Ciara to know I'm hustling."

"It's probably only a matter of time before they find out, you know how tha streets talk."

They won't find out, trust me."

"I hope not, Aunt Zelda would have a baby.

"Who you tellin, I'm about to take a nap I'm tired as shit."

CHAPTER 6

Cal Need Some Work

"Jibbs can I holla at you for a sec?

"Yeah, what tha biz is Cal?"

"I need you to put me on, I'm tired of being broke."

"My Cuz on ya shit?"

"Nah, I just need to step it up, and you tha person to help a nigga to do that."

"What can you handle and don't be fronting."

"Let me start wit 4½ to see how fast I can move that."

"Do you have somewhere to move it?"

"Yeah, I got this spot on 52nd & Spruce."

"A'ight, when you ready?"

"Now, if you ready."

"Cal Imma say this one time and one time only, don't Fuck my money up cause I wouldn't want to put my cuz through tha grief."

"You ain't got to worry about that, I'm straight up."

"For ya sake I hope so. Hold up let me make a quick call."

"Yo Bo…bring me 4½ around."

"Now?"

"No tomorrow…of course now."

"Cal Imma need 5,400 back since, I'm fronting it to you."

"No problem."

"Take ya time, but don't take forever."

When Bo came around I told Cal to get tha work and hit me when it was done.

"Aye Jibbs, we down to tha last brick."

"Damn already?"

"Yeah tha block been doing major numbers."

"I see…let me call my Cuz."

(Tha phone rang 4 times before she answered it.)

"What's up Jibbs, I'm ready for you."

"Damn Cuz, you ain't playin no games; unfortunately I won't be ready til lunchtime tomorrow."

"That's cool, I got enough to hold me down til then. I hit Cal wit some work too."

"Ciara's Cal?"

"Yeah, he came to me for some help."

"Good cause I was going to give you some work to give to him so he can get up and take care of his family."

"I only gave him 4½ to see what he can do and how fast he could move it."

"Well, Imma give you a brick to give him when he's done that."

"Oh yeah, Ciara called to remind me to bring Classy to tha party Saturday."

"Just give him one of those Nintendo Wii's."

"He's too young for that."

"No he's not…when he stays wit Classy they play all tha time."

"What's up wit you? How are you feeling?"

"Exhausted."

"Turn ya phone off and get some sleep."

"That's what I was about to do when you called me."

"My fault…go head to sleep, just hit me when you get up."

"Bo we gotta stretch this until tomorrow."

"That ain't no problem."

CHAPTER 7

Joey's Cousin Parker Dealt Wit

"I don't care who he is if he talkin reckless, he has to be dealt wit ASAP!"

"What was that all about?"

"Jibbs said that Joey's cousin is talkin shit."

"Talkin shit like what?"

"Say'n if he finds out who did this, he's going to kill them."

"So…he doesn't know I did it, so let 'em talk."

"Zell I see through that…he knows and if he doesn't, he assumes."

"Well, why not have Jibbs bring him to tha Warehouse?"

"Good ideal." I called Jibbs and told him to meet me there wit Joey's cousin.

"I'm coming wit you Zoey."

We pulled up to find Jibbs and Parker already there.

"So what is this all about?" Parker asked.

"I don't know…you tell me, you're tha one talking."

"I don't know…

Cutting him off Zell said, "Cut tha bullshit! You said what you said mafucka!"

"Bitch! Who you think you are?"

Pulling out her Cat 9 Zell said, "Call me another Bitch, I dare you!" I didn't say shit, I just looked on.

"Jibbs…what is this all about?"

"I didn't think so you punk mafucka!" He didn't say shit; he just looked at Zell wit murder in his eyes.

"What's tha matter cat got ya tongue?"

I knew I probably wouldn't leave here alive, but I would leave here wit my pride. "You know what, Fuck you Bitch!"

"Excuse me?"

"You heard me, Fuck you! Ha! Ha! Ha!"

Zell pulled her pistol back out, pointed it at Parker's head, and pulled tha trigger.

"Damn Zell this is a new shirt you just messed up."

"Nigga I'll buy you another one."

"Zell you didn't have to kill him."

"I know, but I want you to know I got ya back at all times."

"I already know you do."

"Yeah and now you know I will never tell either."

"Jibbs do something wit his body."

"I got my peeps at tha morgue who'll cremate bodies for me at 5 stacks a body."

"Are you serious?"

"Dead." We all laughed at that.

"Well from now on anytime we need to dispose of anyone that's where they go, then flush tha ashes down tha toilet. Jibbs give ya peeps an extra 3 grand on tha strength."

"I'll call you when everything is done."

"No need, I know you can handle it. I almost forgot, I got something for you, so call when you finish wit this."

"What time does that shipment come in today?"

"It should already be in, I'm on my way to check on that now."

"Zoey, I need to be more hands on."

"No you don't…you a'ight doing what you're doing."

"What counting money?"

"Yup."

"That shit is boring."

"Boring and safe. You really want to get involved wit tha other aspects of this?"

"Yes."

"A'ight I tell you what, you can be my Robin...so to speak."

"I rather not be Robin, he didn't get to do shit but hang out wit Batman."

"Naw, Robin always had his back when Batman fought…so did he.

"Listen Zoey, not only am I ya cousin but I'm also ya best friend."

"Zell you not telling me nothing I don't already know, but I just want to keep you safe."

"You've been keeping me safe all my life, not that I don't appreciate it, but I can stand on my own two feet."

"Fuck it, you want to be all tha way in that's up to you, but know once ya in ain't no turning back."

"I know and I'm in."

CHAPTER 8

Some Good Weed…Cheap!

I woke up to tha smell of marijuana. When I got myself together and went downstairs Zell was smoking a blunt.

"Oh you back smoking?"

"I never stop, plus this is that weed we have been waiting on."

"Well is it any good?"

"This is tha best weed I smoked in a while, it taste like Sour D and Kush mixed."

"Javier said it was some good weed."

"Well he wasn't bullshit'n, how much are we pay'n?"

"500 a pound."

"That's all? We can sell them for 1,500 easy."

"Ain't nobody gonna pay that number."

"Yes they will, they pay 2,500 or better for Exotic."

"I know a lot of people that will jump on this so let me make a few calls right now. If they are paying what you said then we sell them for 2 stacks."

She pulled out her phone, dialed a number, while she was talking she gave me tha thumbs up. She hung up and called a few more people all wit tha same results.

"That went a lot better than I thought, I just sold 60 pounds for $180,000."

"Are you serious?"

"Yup, most of them were spending 4,500, so of course they gonna jump at our number and tha weed is much better."

"I only got a 100 to see how well they would move."

Over tha next two days everything was moving rather quickly, I even had this doctor on tha payroll who was writing us prescriptions of Promethazine (Codeine Syrup) by tha gallons, not to mention Zanies. Jibbs block was now tha 'ONE STOP SHOP' and they were doing stupid numbers.

"Hey Cuz."

"Whats up Zoey?"

"I got this syrup and pills for you."

"Good cause we are running low, this shit is flying off tha shelves. Everybody that was going to Jay Street is coming down here now."

"That's a good thing ain't it?"

"Hell yeah, I'm not complaining."

"I know you not wit tha numbers yall doing down there."

"Yeah, cause I am kinda proud wit tha help of you."

"How I took my block from a small biz-ness to a corporation, so to speak."

"I have to go pick Classy up so we can get to tha party."

"You still got an hour before it starts."

"I know but you know how her mom is."

"Yeah petty…I never liked her."

"Me either," he said laughing…shit just happens.

"Well, I'll see you at tha party."

CHAPTER 9

Happy 4th Birthday Calry

I had to stop and pick tha cake up before going to my mom's. While I was there I grabbed a couple balloons that said Happy 4th Birthday. On my way out tha store I ran into this guy that was always hitting on me in tha club.

"Hello Zoey."

"Hey."

"Sorry about ya loss." I just nodded and kept it moving. Now don't get me wrong, Jason was fine as hell, 6'1, brown eyes, wavy hair, and dark skinned.

"I just was wit Quez. Well I guess I'll see you around."

"Maybe," I said getting into my car.

There was an accident so I had to take another route to my mom's.

"I didn't think you was going to make it."

"No they had a big accident on Broad, so I had to come tha long way."

"How you feeling?"

"OK I guess."

"Aunt Zoey!" my nephew said running up to me.

"Hey Happy Birthday you." He was all smiles.

"I'm 4," he said holding up 3 fingers.

"You need 1 more finger up."

"Oh snap!"

"Boy you so crazy," I said giving him a big hug.

While my mom cooked we all played 'Pin tha Tail on tha Donkey' and all tha other games Ciara brought to entertain a bunch of toddlers.

"A'ight who's ready to eat?"

"Me! Me! Me!" they all yelled at tha top of their lungs.

"Mom did you make those special meatballs?"

"Yes I did and I also made party wings, macaroni salad, and corn on tha cobb."

"Oooooooh Mom-Mom my favorite!"

"I know Baby that's why Mom-Mom made it."

Once tha kids were done eating it was time to sing Happy Birthday and cut tha cake.

"A'ight everybody on tha count of three, 1, 2, 3...Happy Birthday to you, Happy Birthday to you, Happy Birthday Calry, Happy Birthday to you!" When he blew out tha candles all tha kids screamed.

"Cal did you get it?" Ciara asked.

"Of course I got it, did you get it?"

"Yup."

My sister was tha type that wanted everything on tape and camera.

"Mommy can I open my presents now?"

"Don't you want to eat ya cake and ice cream first?"

"No!"

"Well you are because once you open ya stuff you ain't gonna wanna eat." Calry looked at me wit that auntie help me face.

"Ciara, if he wants to open his stuff, let him."

"I know Cuz," Jibbs added then winked at Calry.

"I can see I'm not going to win this fight, so come on." We all headed to tha family room.

"First present is from Aunt Zoey."

When he saw tha clothes he said, "Aunty you know how I like to style." After opening most of his gifts which were clothes, he got to Jibbs gift.

"Yeeeesss! Yeeeesss!" he yelled jumping up and down after seeing tha Wii.

"Thanks Classy," he said giving her a big hug.

When Cal came in wit tha Escalade Power Wheel sittin on 24's he went bananas, "Oh Shiiiit!"

"Boy you better watch ya Damn mouth!"

"I know that's right Cal," said tapping him on his head.

"Ow Daddy."

I looked at Cal and smiled, ever since we gave him that work a few days ago he's been doing his thing. I don't know if he sold that brick wholesale or not, cause he offed it in 2 days.

"Jibbs let me holla at you real quick."

"What up Cal?"

"Yo, I need some more work."

"Damn you done that shit already?"

"I don't hold grams."

"A'ight I'll get wit you after this."

"Cool."

"What you smiling about?"

"Cal ain't playin no games, he's done already."

"When did you give him tha work?"

"Yesterday."

"He has to be selling weight."

"One of my young boys did say that he had 52nd Street jumping again."

"Oh shit that's where he set up shop?"

"Yeah why?"

"Miles told me that somebody had 52nd & Spruce doing dumb numbers in less than a week."

"That's Cal."

"Look, ask him how many can he dump in a week, then let me know."

"What are you two over there talkin about?"

"Biz-ness."

"I should have known…Aunt Zelda is looking for yall."

"Come on before she sends out tha Coast Guards."

It was 6 o'clock by tha time tha party was over Calry asked Jibbs if Classy could stay tha night.

"You didn't even ask ya mom little nigga."

"Oh yeah mom can she?"

"I don't care, Jibbs just make sure you bring her some clothes back."

"A'ight Imma do that now."

"Just drop them at my house, I'll be there."

"Zoey, I hollered at Cal and he said he didn't know. Just give him 3 days and we'll go from there."

CHAPTER 10

Zoacis Styles & Cutz

I sat up in tha bed awake from tha dream I just had about Quez. It has been 6 months since Quez was killed, over tha last 2 months I've been having these dreams about him.

I jumped in tha shower and got dressed. I had invested some money into stocks which was doing pretty well. I was even thinking about opening a beauty salon to give my little cousin a job, she was doing hair out of my aunt's house.

I walked in and there were people everywhere.

"Hey Cuz."

"Damn Acis you've got it poppin in here."

"I know ever since I won that hair competition biz-ness has skyrocketed."

"You doing all these heads?"

"Yeah and I got a lot more to do after these."

"You need to be in somebody's shop."

"Hell no, then I would have to pay somebody for a chair, thanks but no thanks."

"Listen, how would you like to work for me?"

"Doing what?"

"Hair, what else?"

"Where?"

"I'm thinking about opening a unisex salon and you'll be running it."

"So I'll work for you, but everybody else will work for me."

"Yup."

"When do I start?"

"Tha shop won't be ready for another 3 to 6 months."

"Well count me in."

"I knew you would be interested."

"Hell yeah! And we can call it Zoacis Styles & Cutz."

"Hmmm…I might be able to work wit that."

"Do you know any stylist or barbers?"

"Yes I do."

"I mean top notch."

"Zoey now you're being disrespectful."

"I'm try'n to knock all tha competition out tha box."

"When I was in college I met some people that can work some hair, male and female."

"Well call them up and let them know it's on. Zoacis is going to blow tha comp up like tha Twin Towers. I'll call you; I have to go meet wit tha designers."

CHAPTER 11

Pit Tried to Set Me Up!

"Yo what tha deal Cal?"

"Same shit, different smell."

"What's good wit you though?"

"I need one of those Sweet Potato Pies ya peeps be making ASAP."

"No problem, I got one fresh out of tha oven for you."

"Do I need to come and get it or do you want to bring it to me?"

"How about we meet in tha middle."

"Sounds good…see you in 15."

"Make sure you got 33 dollars, last time you only gave me 31."

"I know that's why I got 35; these are tha best in tha city. So I gotta make sure I keep you square."

"Box I need you to follow me."

"Who was that…Pit?"

"Yeah."

"Cal, if you don't trust him why you keep Fuckin wit him?"

"Because his money is good."

"Always go wit ya first instinct."

I jumped in tha car, on my way I thought about what Box said and he was right. This would be my last time Fuckin wit Pit. I pulled up but told Box to keep going, as soon as I pulled in, police and vice came from everywhere.

"Put ya hands on tha Fuckin steering wheel!"

As soon as I did another cop snatched me out tha car.

"Yo, what tha Fuck is going on?"

"You know what's going on, don't try and play dumb!" While tha cops where searching tha car, Box rode pass.

"Sarg there's nothing here but some pies."

"Where are tha drugs?"

"Drugs? I don't sell no drugs, I sale Sweet Potato Pies."

"Bullshit! We got a tip that you would be meeting somebody here wit a brick of coke."

"That's bullshit! I was supposed to meet somebody but wit a pie not no drugs." Tha police just looked at each other pissed off.

"Can I please go? I have to deliver tha rest of these pies."

"Take tha cuffs off him."

"Sorry for tha mix up," tha Sarg said with an obvious attitude.

As I was getting in my car, I saw Pit try'n to duck down in tha police car. I acted as if I didn't see him.

"Hello."

"I told you."

"I know but that's why I always have you follow me wit tha work and I keep these pies on deck."

"You straight?"

"Yeah, meet me at tha house I need to call Jibbs."

"You must be physic, I was just about to call you."

"Is that right?"

"Yeah."

"Well I heard you just had a run in wit Philly's finest."

"Yeah, that mafucka Pit tried to set me up."

"What happened?"

"This nigga called and wanted a pie, so I told him where to be and come straight this time because last time he was short on tha Sweet Potato Pie."

"Sweet Potato Pie?"

"Yeah, I have all my peoples call for them just in case something like this happens."

"So what happen when you got there?"

"Tha cops swarmed me, and searched me and my car."

"They didn't find tha work?"

"Wasn't no work to be found, I never ride dirty."

"So what would have happened if he wasn't try'n to set you up?"

"I would have gotten his money and told him where to pick it up at.

And when tha cops saw that there was only pies in tha car, they were pissed."

"So you really had pies?"

"Hell yeah, I keep them."

"You a lot smarter than I thought."

"Tha funny thing, when I was leaving Pit was ducking down in tha cop car. I acted like I didn't see him."

"Good, let me deal wit him. I don't want you involved wit this."

"Jibbs no disrespect, but tha nigga just tried to book me a long stay at Graterford, so I need to handle this."

"I understand, but don't you think tha cops will know it was you? Let me handle it, he'll never be seen or heard from again, I promise."

"You know what I'll do for you; I'll let you help me kill him."

"Now we talkin."

"Meet me at this address 8 o'clock sharp."

"How you gonna get him to come?"

"Let me worry about that, you just meet me at that address."

"No more said."

CHAPTER 12

The Rat Pit is Poisoned, Tortured and Killed

"Zoey do you still have Pits number?"

"I don't think so why?" I explained tha situation to her.

"Hold on...let me check my phone. Nope I don't got it but I know who might...hold on *(Chirp)*

"What up Zoey?" *(Chirp)*

"Do you still got Pit number? *(Chirp)*

"I was just about to delete it, why, what's up?" *(Chirp)*

"I need you to call him and tell him you want a date." *(Chirp)*

"A date?" *(Chirp)*

"Just do it and hit me right back!" *(Chirp)*

"OK...Jibbs."

"Yeah, I'm still here."

"That's good shit Cal got going on wit those pies."

"I know," we said tha same time.

"Shit! *(Chirp) (Chirp)* that's Zell, hold up." *(Chirp)*

"He's picking me up at 7 o'clock." *(Chirp)*

"A'ight...thank you Zell." *(Chirp)*

"Ain't you gonna tell me what's going on?" *(Chirp)*

"Yes I'm gonna tell you. I'm on my way over." *(Chirp)*

"OK Jibbs meet me at Zell's."

"Be there in 15."

Me and Zoey pulled up at tha same time.

"So who's going to tell me what this is all about?"

"I'll let you do tha honors Jibbs."

"Long story short, Pit is a RAT, he tried to set Cal up."

"What? Are you serious?"

"So what do you want me to do?"

"Nothing, we just needed you to get him to come over."

"I don't want that Rat in my house."

"Once he gets here invite him in, we'll do tha rest. Actually, I need you to offer him a drink and pour this in it," Jibbs said handing her a vial wit some type of liquid inside.

When Zell's phone rang she picked it up then said, "It's him."

"Answer it and invite him in."

"Hello. Hey Pit can you come in for a minute, I'm not quite ready yet."

He came to tha front door and walked in wit out knocking.

"Next time knock first."

"Oh my fault, I thought you wanted me to just walk in."

"Would you like something to drink?"

"Sure."

"Water or juice?"

"Do you have some Remy?"

"Yeah, hold up." As I was pouring his drink I asked if he wanted ice.

"No I like my drinks straight, no ice no chaser."

"I heard that," I said slipping tha liquid that Jibbs gave me in.

"Here you go, I'll be right back." I walked into my bedroom where Jibbs and Zoey were.

"How long does it take for that stuff to work?"

"10 minutes." We all walked out to find Pit slumped over.

"Come open tha door so I can put him in tha van."

"What about his car?"

"Put some gloves on and drive it to tha bad lands. Leave tha keys in tha ignition and leave it running. Zoey we go wit her so she can get back, I'll handle this Rat."

It was 7:45 am when I pulled up to tha funeral home. I was surprised to see Cal already there. He flicked his high beams when he spotted me. I motioned for him to get out and help me wit Pit.

"Damn this mafucka is heavy." Once we got him inside we took him down to tha basement.

"I need to get my bag out of tha car."

"Hurry up." By tha time Cal came back Pit was coming around.

"Where tha hell am I?"

"Now that's not important here, but what is, is that shit you tried to do today wit my man Cal."

"Who's Cal? I don't know no Fuckin Cal!"

"Oh so now you don't know me?" Cal asked stepping out of tha shadows. He didn't say shit.

"That's what I thought nigga. Now Pit answer me this, what did I ever do to you for you to want to see me in jail?"

"I don't know what you're talkin bout'" *(SMACK!)*

"Nigga you had tha Jakes waiting on me today."

Cal went into his bag and pulled out an axe.

"Tha only way to stop you from calling tha police would be to do this." *(WACK!)*

"Aaaaaaahhh Shiiiiiiiiit, Aaaaaaaahhh!"

"Was that tha hand you called tha cops wit you Rat Mafucka? Huh? Or was it this one?" *(WACK!)*

"Aaaaaaahhh Fuuuuuck!" I watched as Cal slowly tortured Pit. When I finally had seen enough, I pulled out my 45 and shot him in tha head.

"I guess I was takin too long?"

"Nah I just got other shit to do."

"So where are we going to dump tha body?"

"Right here."

"Oh we going to bury him huh?"

"Nah."

"Now you lost me." Roy came in and asked if I was ready.

"Yeah lets get this shit over wit, I got a hot date tonight."

When we were done, I gave tha ashes to Cal and told him to flush them.

"Nah Imma spread them in tha streets."

"I don't care what you do wit them as long as you get rid of 'em."

"Damn this is tha sweetest way to get rid of a mafucka and not get caught."

"Yeah, but this shit doesn't leave this room or I'll be flushing ya ashes...CAPICE?"

"If you don't know by now that you can trust me then I guess you neva will."

"I don't trust my own mom!" I left wit a newfound respect for Cal; I knew that he was down for tha cause by any means necessary.

CHAPTER 13

LT and Rosco Plotting to Take tha City Over

LT I'm telling you, we need to find out who she's copping from and take this shit over."

"You need to be patient."

"I didn't run Quez down just to have his Bitch take over."

"I know that's why we need to speed tha process up."

"Rosco you're not seeing tha big picture."

"And what's that?"

"We let her get her money up then we kill her and tha city is ours."

"Nigga that shit could take a year, maybe longer."

"So tha Fuck what?"

"What ever man."

"Nigga you act like we're hurting for money."

"That's not tha point; we got rid of that mafucka Quez for us to take over tha city, not his Bitch."

"Rosco just be patient our time will come and when it does tha whole town will know."

"LT I trust you, I just want what we worked so hard to get."

"I know you do but in tha meantime we're going to continue to get at a dollar until it's time to strike and we find out just who's on her side."

CHAPTER 14

At Ms. Tootsies Discussing Biz-ness

"Zoey my man Jax called me and said he wanted me to meet a couple of his peeps."

"His peeps who?"

"Some cats named Rosco and LT."

"LT?"

"Yeah you know him?"

"Not personally, but I remember Quez said he didn't trust him and he would never do biz-ness wit him."

"No more said, I'm not dealing wit him."

"Did you eat yet?"

"Nah."

"Why don't you join me and Zell for lunch at Ms. Tootsies at 12 o'clock?"

"A'ight, is it cool if I bring Bo along?"

"That's up to you."

"Yo what's up wit ya cousin, she still messing wit that nigga Spence?"

"Why nigga?"

"I was just asking."

"Don't even think about it."

"Nigga I ain't say nothing when you was knocking my peoples off."

"Yeah but if you would've, I would've fell back."

"If I did, you wouldn't have that beautiful daughter of yours."

"True dat."

"Come on let's go in before Zoey starts blowing my phone up."

"I was just about to call you." Me and Bo looked at one another and busted out laughing.

"What's so funny?"

"I know, did we miss tha joke?"

"Nah, I just told Bo that we better get in here before you start calling."

"Nah nigga you said before she starts blowing ya phone up."

"Oh did he?"

"Anyway hey Zell, hey Zoey?"

"Boy sit down so we can order because a Bitch is starving."

After we ordered we discussed a little bit of biz-ness.

"So Zell do you still talk to Spence?"

"Yes."

"Is he coming out this year."

"He said he was."

"I think that he made tha right decision last year to stay one more year."

"Me too cause he was tha best thing moving this year."

"Not to mention he play for Roy Williams at North Carolina, it's like they breed ball prayers in Chapel Hill."

"Except for when Carmelo Anthony did it for tha Orangemen, no other freshman has took their team all tha way and won a title."

"If he goes first he'll be play'n out of Memphis wit A.I." When our food came, we didn't waste no time diggin in.

"Jibbs what tha deal is?"

"I can't call it, what's good wit you?"

"Same shit different smell, this my man LT and Roscoe I was telling you about."

"Oh yeah."

"Yeah, I know yall enjoying yall lunch so I'll call you and we can talk biz-ness."

"Oh about that, Imma fall back for now."

"Damn I ain't never seen a mafucka that ain't want to get no real paper."

"I'm small time, I probably couldn't handle ya order any way Big Bank."

"I know that's right," LT said walking off.

When I was sure they were outta ear shot I said, "I see why Quez didn't trust 'em."

"Yo that nigga Rosco looks like tha nigga that shot Lli Mikey a few months back."

"Ask Lil Mikey tha nigga name that hit him, if that is him he will be dealt wit.

We finished our lunch and went our separate ways.

CHAPTER 15

BLING…Ciara's Ring

"I'm telling you Zoey those two niggaz are going to be trouble."

"I'm not even tha least bit worried about them if they know what's best they better stay in their lane."

"Did you see tha way tha one that called himself LT was looking at you?"

"I peeped him."

"I'm telling you Cuz something ain't right wit 'em."

"I'll give you a call later I have a few errands to run."

"OK, I have to stop by Ciara's to see this ring Cal got for her."

"It's beautiful, I saw it earlier when I stopped by to drop off tha shirt he wanted."

"Oooh yall wearing each other's clothes…that's so ghetto."

"Ain't nobody wearing nobody's clothes, I had on a shirt she liked so I bought her one."

"Oh I was gonna say."

"You know Spence will be home this weekend."

"Thats whats up, so I know I won't be seeing you then."

"He said he has a surprise for me, but I already know who's going to tell me he's going pro."

"Well still act like you're surprised and excited."

"Girl you know I am, you don't have to tell me."

I rang tha bell 3 times before somebody finally answered.

"Damn Bitch, what tha hell was you doing...Fuckin?" Ciara didn't say shit, but she didn't have to it was all all over her face.

"You so nasty."

"That's not nasty, its life, besides you said you wouldn't be here til 2 o'clock'

"What time do you think it is?"

"I don't know, sex Ciara time maybe?"

"Ha! Ha! Ha! Girl you funny, now let me see this ring so I can leave and you can get back to biz-ness."

"BLING," she said holding up her hand.

"Wow that is really nice, looks like Cal spent a few dollars on that. So, when is tha wedding?"

"I don't know."

"Well, don't wait too long cause tomorrow is not promised."

"Bye Sis." I turned to leave before tha tears made their way down my face.

"Zoey."

"Yes."

"I love you and I'm always here for you."

"I know, and I love you too."

CHAPTER 16

Zoey Finds Out that Quez was Murdered

After stopping by Ciara's, I just wanted to go home and take a nap. I ended up pulling out tha photo album and thinking about Quez. I miss him so much it hurts, I've been try'n to stay busy so I wouldn't think about him. Next thing I knew, I was balling my eyes out uncontrollably.

"Love so many things I've got to tell you. But I'm afraid I don't know how. Cause there's a possibility you'll look at me differently. Love, ever since the first moment I spoke your name from then on I knew that by you being in my life things were destined to change cause Love."

This was Quez's favorite song he would listen to this song over and over and over again. I turned tha stereo down and caught tha last ring on tha phone. Damn, oh well if it was important they'll call back and sure enough they did.

"Hello."

"Hello, Ms. Brown?"

"Yes, this is she."

"This is Detective Shaw."

"How may I help you detective?"

"I have some new information on ya fiancé case."

"You found tha drunk driver?"

"No because there was no drunken driver, Quez, was murderd."

"Murdered!"

"Yes, we found tha car that was used to run him down."

"How do you know that he was murdered?"

"Because tha car was reported stolen and its tha same car our witness saw leaving tha scene. That's all I have for now, but I will find tha killer or killers. Ms. Brown, are you still there?"

"Yes, I'm just at a lost for words."

"Do you know of anybody that would want him dead?"

"No, he didn't have any ememies."

"Well, I'll keep you updated."

"Thank you, Detective."

"It's my job and if you come across anything that would be helpful, please don't hesitate to call."

After I hung up I called Javier to inform him of tha new developments.

"My son was what?"

"That's tha same thing I said, Javier did he memtion anything to you about beefing wit anyone?"

"No, but he did say he had heard about a couple of guys who wanted his spot, but I can't recall tha names. I'm going to put my ear to tha streets and see what I can find out."

"Zoey, I want in when you find out and I know you will. You got that? I also put tha dogs in tha cage."

"Ok, I'll pick them up in a few hours."

We have to talk in code since we weren't on our burn outs. I needed to lay down, I had a splitting headache.

CHAPTER 17

Zoacis Styles & Cutz Grand Opening

It has been 3 weeks since I had gotten that call from Detective Shaw, and I still haven't heard anything as of yet. I was on my way to meet wit Alex at tha shop to see if everything meets my standards. I had a thousand fliers printed out, so they could be passed out all over Philly for tha Grand Opening next week. I walked into tha shop and my mouth dropped open.

"Well, say something."

"Alex, I love it, it's just like I wanted it."

Barbers on one side, stylist on tha other, big screen TV's in 4 corners and in tha waiting room, marble floor wit Zoacis in tha middle, but what I really loved was tha kids room. I had that put in just in case they couldn't get a babysitter, they could bring them wit 'em.

I sat down in one of tha chairs, "OOOOh, these are so soft and comfortable."

"Just like you wanted, so tha customer can be comfortable while they get their hair done or cut."

I immediately got on tha phone to call Acis, so she could inform everybody that tha shop would be open in 5 days and to hand out tha fliers. I ended up getting another thousand made. By tha time we were done, all of Philly knew about ZOACIS STYLES & CUTZ.

I was at tha shop at 6 that morning for tha Grand Opening. We had a receptionist to make tha appointments and inform tha stylist when their appointments were in, we only did walk-ins on Mondays, Tuesdays and Wednesdays tha other 3 days were appointment only. Me and Acis cut tha ribbon together and Zoacis Styles & Cutz we're officially opened.

"Damn doesn't look like this is no Grand Opening look like yall been open for years."

"I know this is a better turnout than I expected."

"This has to be tha best shop in tha city, what other shop can you take ya kids to while you get ya shit done?"

Ciara walked in wit my nephew. "Aunty," he said running to me.

"Boy you need something done wit this hair."

"I washed it and didn't have time to braid it cause I was running late. I'll do it when I get home."

"Don't worry about it Lisa, how many heads you got?"

"3 but I'll slide him in next, it won't take me long to hook him up."

After 30 minutes Lisa had my nephews' hair strapped.

"Mommy, Mommy look what Ms. Lisa did," he said turning his head around so Ciara could see.

"Wow Lisa you are tha shit. How much do I owe you?"

"Don't worry about it Sis, I got it."

"Well I still need to know what she charge so Calry can be in her chair every two weeks."

"Just 20 dollars." I could tell my nephew really liked it because he wouldn't stay out of tha mirror. While Ciara was talking to me my phone went off.

"Whats up Jibbs?"

"I need to see you yesterday. Where you at?"

"Tha shop."

"Oh shit, today is tha Grand Opening I'm on my way."

"I'm feeling this," I said as I walked into tha crowded salon.

"Jibbs what tha deal is?"

I turned to see who's talking.

"Damn was you gon' let a mafucka know you switched shops?"

"It was a last minute thing."

"Yeah, but my appointment is in an hour."

"Nigga you would of hit my phone to say you was running late like you do every Saturday." All I could do was laugh cause he was right.

"Jibbs where's Classy?"

"She wit her mom, wow who did ya hair, ya mom?"

"No, Ms. Lisa," he said pointing to tha girl who was hooking up another dude.

"Damn Ma, you got skills, can I get in tha chair next?"

"Yeah, but I just got to put some straight backs in his hair, but that won't take but a second."

"A'ight, so where is Zoey?"

"In her office," Acis said.

"Hey Big Head, you finally got a shop and biz-ness is booming on tha first day."

"You need to tell ya Baby Mom to bring Classy."

"That would be like playing tha Powerball."

"I know right, Aunt Thelma supposed to come by later."

"Taz, Imma get my wig done first."

"That's cool you know I got you." Taz was one of, if not tha best barbers in Philly.

"Nice real nice," I said walking in Zoey's office.

"Thank you, but next time knock first."

"My fault Cuz."

"So what's so important?"

"I know some people who know some people that are interested in purchasing 50 bricks."

"Is everything on tha up and up?"

"Yeah, my peeps want 25 and their peeps want tha same."

"As long as shit is cool then handle ya biz."

"I just wanted to let you know because that's tha last of it.

"'Fuck' I been so busy wit tha salon I haven't been on top of it."

"I told you 2 days ago that we needed to re-up on everything."

"I know, but I've just been so busy between tha salon and try'n to find out who killed Quez."

"How's that going anyway?"

"Nothing as of yet, matter of fact, let me call Javier right now."

"You need to introduce us so I can stay on top of this for you."

"I might as well since you're taking care of everything anyway."

"Your absolutely right about that, so turn me on to tha plug, I thought to myself, but said, "we family, that's what family does."

After a few minutes on tha phone wit Javier, everything was set up.

"What did he say?"

"He was coming this way so we're doing lunch tomorrow."

"Can we do dinner?" I gave him look that said are you serious?

"No disrespect, but I have to take Classy to tha doctors tomorrow at 11:30."

"Well, I have to check to see how long he's going to be in town. Why can't her mom take her?"

"Zoey, you already know how she is, too good to get on tha bus."

"How can a Bitch be too good when she doesn't own a car?"

"I was thinking about buying her a Honda or some type of hoopty."

"Why?"

"So she won't have an excuse why she can't do things, plus I won't have to do it."

"Well in that case, I saw a nice car at tha auction tha other day."

"Now what were you doing at tha auction?"

"I went to get Acis a car."

"Is that where you got that Lexus 400 from?"

"Yup, and I only paid $4,500 for it."

"How does it run?"

"Like a champ, most of those cars were confiscated from drug dealers."

"So what days do they hold tha auctions anyway?"

"Monday thru Friday from 8 to 8 and Saturdays from 11 to 6."

"Let me get Bo so I can shoot up there now, I'll hit you later."

"OK"

After Jibbs left I called Javier to see how long he would be in town for. Once our conversation was done I walked back into tha salon and it was jam packed.

"Maybe I should have brought a bigger place."

"I don't know, but we gonna make a lot of paper," Acis said wit a big smile.

"Why yall don't have tha TV's or radio on?"

"Cause don't nobody knows how to work it," Taz said. I turned tha TV on video, but turned it down because I had Jay-Z's Blueprint 3 playing.

"Turn it up some Cuz."

I looked around tha shop and smiled...pleased wit tha outcome of our first day. There was no doubt in my mind that tha salon would be a major success.

CHAPTER 18

Tha Auction

"Yo LT did you tell Kyle to holla at his man Jibbs again?"

"Yeah, he said he will give him a call today."

"I know he gonna Fuck wit us, he'd be a fool to turn down this money."

"I know cause I don't care how much money you got, ain't nobody in their right mind turning down 150 grand."

"Yo, this Kyle right here."

"Yo, tell me something good."

"I set up a meeting wit Jibbs at 3 o'clock." I looked at my watch, "Damn, nigga thats in 30 minutes, why you just now calling?"

"I had some shit I had to handle."

"Kyle if you wasn't my dad's nephew, you might be in tha bottom of tha ocean."

"Ha! Ha! Ha! Well, I guess I'm one lucky nigga then."

"Where do we need to be?"

"Tha auction."

"Tha auction?"

"Yeah, he's already there, that's why he said meet him there."

25 minutes later we were pulling up to tha auto auction.

"Ain't that him over there?"

"Where?"

"Right there standing by that Park Ave."

Jibbs my cousin Kyle yelled out, "Nigga, all that money you got and you at tha auction!"

"I'm getting my daughter's mom a car so she can leave me alone."

"This is a nice whip."

"I know I got my mechanic making sure ain't nothing wrong wit it."

"How much they want for this?"

"5 stacks."

"Damn, that's cheap, this is a 04?"

"Shit, I'm going to even grab that ES 300 over there for my trap car."

"Enough about this, here's tha deal, my cousin doesn't want to deal wit yall because Quez didn't trust yall."

"Man Fuck that bitch ass nigga, that's why he is where he is."

"I'm not tha type of nigga to pass up no money."

"Now that's what we talkin bout."

"So how many do you need and when?"

"We need 8 right now."

"As soon as I'm done here, I'll be right at yall."

"We got tha doe wit us, so you might as well take it, that way you just have to drop tha work off."

"How about this? Let me make a call and I can have it here in tha next 30 to 45 minutes."

"Hey that's even better."

"Give me ya number and as soon as it gets here I'll hit you."

"That's what it is and in tha meantime we gon' to look around."

"Rosco I told you that nigga wasn't no fool. First we gon' blow, then we're going to take over tha town," I said giving Rosco some dap.

"Now we're getting somewhere finally," Roscoe said wit a smile on his face like a kid on Christmas day. I ended up buying a 94 Caprice that needed a little work, but nothing that I our presidents couldn't handle.

(MONEY MONEY MONEY IS MY BITCH)

"Yo," I said answering my phone.

"Is tha doe in ya car?"

"Yeah."

"What kind of car and can you unlock tha door from there?"

"Tha white Acura on dueces and tha money is under tha drivers seat."

"A'ight, by tha time you get out of there tha coke will be in tha same spot."

"OK. Oh by tha way, nice car you just purchased."

"Thanks and we'll be getting at you when we're done."

"No doubt, take ya time and be safe."

CHAPTER 19

Handlin Biz-ness

We walked inside tha Stash House ready to get down to biz-ness.

"I hope this is as good as they say it is."

"We bout to find out right now." I dropped 9 into tha pot adding 80 grams of baking soda turning it into 12½ ounces.

"Old Man Skip come try this out for me."

I broke him off a nice 20, Old Man Skip was tha type of nigga that he didn't care who you were or how much money you had, if ya shit wasn't no good, he was gonna let you know. When Old Man Skip came back his mouth was twisted. He didn't have to say it because I already knew by his face it was Grade A stuff.

"Young'n you got something on ya hands wit that, I ain't had nothin that good since tha 80's. Now you could put something on it, but I would leave it just like it is." What Old Man Skip didn't know was, I had already turned 9 into 12½ and it was still fire.

"Rosco did you get in touch wit tha young boys from Delaware?"

"Yeah, I told them when I called to meet us in Chester at tha same spot."

"Good, we can give 'em 2 for 70 grand." Once we finished we headed to Ducky's Spot to put tha work in and handle B.I.

"Since we gotta go to Chester, let me hit my man and let him know everything is a go." We had clientele in Philly, but Chester and Delaware were where we got tha most money.

"Damn, we only got 3 left, you need to hit Jibbs up again."

"I'm already on top of that," I said holding my phone to my ear.

"Jibbs, what tha deal is? Everything was on point, right?"

"For sho, I need to place another order."

"Damn Baby, you ain't playin no games, I see."

"I don't hold them grams."

"I see."

"I need another 24 if you got it."

"I got what ever ya money can afford."

"Now see, that's what I'm talkin bout."

"You already ready now?"

"Give me an hour, I need to handle something first."

"No problem, do you and hit me when you ready and we can go from there."

"Will do."

After hanging up, we headed to Chester to handle biz-ness.

"You need to talk to ya man, if he keep coming up short on that money I'm gonna have to handle him."

"No need for that Cal, I took care of that already."

"I hope so."

"I'll let him keep his shit in my Ducky Boy's Spot, that way, his mom won't be able to steal shit. I'm about to run this shit in shifts wit a runner, a money man, and lookouts."

"That's some good shit."

"Tha workers might not like it, but they'll be getting paid at tha end of tha week."

"That might be what they need so they can start stacking their paper."

"Yeah, cause as much paper as this block."

"See ain't no way everybody shouldn't be up."

"Who you tellin, we run thru at least 5 birds a week and that's on a bad week."

"My point exactly."

"These young boys need some guidance. Box by tha time I'm done, this whole block will be on top."

"Cal, we all need a little help sometimes."

"Don't I know, you don't have to tell me. A few months ago I was struggling to get on top, but wit tha help of my folk, now look at me."

"Thanks to you my nigga I'm on top too."

"Box you my nigga, ain't no way I'm going to be on top and you not.How would that shit look? Only a selfish nigga would do some shit like that."

"That's why I got a lot of respect for you Cal and tha fact that we go back like bell bottoms and platform shoes."

"Ha! Ha! Ha! Nigga you crazy as a mafucka. But on some real shit, I need you to get everybody together so I could put them down wit tha new game plan."

"Give me about an hour."

"A'ight, meet me in Ms. Wilma's house."

CHAPTER 20

Ms. Wilma's House and Tha Bet

I sat in Ms. Wilma's house waiting on tha rest of tha squad to arrive.

Box walked in wit Glass and KC and he asked, "This everybody?"

"Yeah."

"Now that we're all here, let me explain why I needed to see you all."

After I had explained to everyone how it would be, and who would be doing what, and working what shifts, they all seemed to be OK wit it.

"Now does anybody have any questions or any complaints?"

"No, I just want to say let's get this money," my young boy Tweek said.

"Damn Cal, we only been doing this for 2 weeks and we already seeing way more money."

"I hope you are stacking ya money."

"Come on, I've been doing that since you put me on," Tweek said wit a smile.

"That's why I Fucks wit you, you ain't no dumb nigga. Don't get me wrong KC and Glass are my peeps, but they don't know how to stack."

"I see they done grabbed up cars and jewels. Wit me I need to be all tha way up when I grab a whip or some bait mafucka's gonna know I'm bout my biz-ness."

"Now that's what I'm talkin bout a little nigga. Do you got ya license?"

"Of course, I'm not driving wit out it. Cal I ain't no dumb young boy."

"I know, you're proving that, Tweek in tha next few months you gonna have so much money you ain't going to know what to do wit it."

"Invest."

"What?"

"Imma invest in some legal shit, clean tha dirty money up. Like last week I went to AC."

"Oh you gamble?"

"Hell naw, I went to get a cashier's check so I could put tha money in tha bank wit out arousing attention."

"Tweek you are very smart because a 5 grand check they wouldn't question it," I said just to see what he would say.

"Nah Cal 5 stacks I could have just put that in there wit no problem. You know 10 stacks is when they start to question, so how would I drop 50 stacks wit out them callin da boys.

"You dropped 50 g's."

"Yeah and another 5 this morning."

"Damn Baby Boy, you have been stacking ya chips."

"I got a lot more, but I know I can't keep getting cashier checks."

"My Uncle has a landscape biz-ness, so I was going to pay him so that he could give me a $50,000 check."

"You holding like that?"

"I've been going hard for 6 months, so why wouldn't my doe be up, not to mention tha grinding I was doing before we hooked up."

"Listen Cal, no disrespect I know that this is ya block and I would never step on ya toes, but I want to grab a little work off of you and wit ya approval knock it off on Sundays, since that's tha day we all have off."

All I could do was smile because I knew that Tweek was on his way to be a boss of his own and who was I to stand in his way.

"Sure you could do that."

"Well, since tomorrow is Sunday could I grab something today?"

"Sure, what you need?"

"How much for a bird?"

I had to think since Jibbs was charging me 30, I didn't want to charge him too much so I said, "35."

"That's it?"

"Yeah, but if you want I could charge you more."

"Nah, but I do want it raw."

"You know how to whip?"

"Of course."

"Don't try to step on it and mess tha work up."

"Trust me no disrespect, but it's gonna be better than ya work."

"I hear you little nigga. Well KC shift is over at 12, so it's all you after that. I'm going to go grab tha work and meet you at Ms. Wilma's."

"A'ight, cause I gotta go get tha money."

Later after I turned 36 ounces into 50; I decided to break off instead of bagging up. Actually, I had Ms. Wilma bagging up while I broke off until she was finished. At first, nobody wanted tha break off because they thought they were getting less. In all actuality, they were, is was tha fact that I was taking shorts that made them buy it.

"Yo Tweek, this ain't tha usual shit you be having."

"You don't like it?"

"Hell no, I love it, yall need to put this on tha block all tha time," a smile instantly came across my face as I told Cal.

Next thing I knew, junkies were coming from all over to get my work by then I was back to tha bags.

It was 5 in tha morning when Ms. Wilma said that there were only 300 dimes left. I couldn't believe it, I ran through 48½ ounces in 5 hours, I called Cal to see if I could score again.

"Yo what up Tweek is everything cool?"

"Yeah, I need another one."

"Get tha Fuck outta here, you done already?"

"Just about, man they're coming from everywhere to get this good shit I whipped up."

"I'll be thru in 30 minutes."

"Damn thats long?"

"Make it 15."

"Now that's what I'm talking bout."

When I pulled up, tha block was jumping like it was a block party. I went in Ms. Wilma's house to wait for Tweek.

"Hey Cal."

"Hey."

"I think you need to let Tweek cook ya shit from now on. "

"Why is that?"

"You don't see all those people out there?"

"How could I miss 'em?"

"I'm telling you, it's been like that for tha last 5 hours and it doesn't look like they gon let up no time soon."

Tweek came in, "Yo here's tha money." He wasted no time dropping tha whole bird in tha pot witin minutes he was done.

"That's how you cook a bird," he said smiling at Cal.

"What up little nigga? I told you."

"Yeah, you definitely did."

"Don't worry, I'm not going to call you til about 12 o'clock."

"Call me as much as you need to."

For tha next few hours it was more of tha same thing, junkies flooding tha block. It was one of those days that I knew I would make a lot of money because as crazy it may sound, but tha later it got, tha more money came.

"Cal, Tweek got tha block jumping for a Sunday."

"I know he's been calling me all night. Since when did we start running shifts on Sundays?"

"We didn't, this is all him, we was busting it and he asked if you could do his thing on Sundays so that he could get his doe all tha way up."

"KC and Glass need to be more like him."

"Box I gotta be honest, he's a lot smarter than I gave him credit for."

"I don't know, but tha block don't even be jumping like this for us."

"Ms. Wilma said that they love tha way he cooks his shit up. Tha way he got 'em lined up, I know he ran through at least a jawn."

"When I tell you this you're not going to believe it, if I didn't bring it to him, I probably wouldn't even believe it."

"I'm listening."

"He ran thru 3 birds, this is his 4th one."

"Get tha Fuck outta here nigga!"

"I'll swear on everything, he got friends from all over Philly pulling up to get his coke. My young boy don't play no games." I didn't mention to him about tha money Tweek put in tha bank, because I could be wrong, but I thought I saw a little bit of jealousy.

"Well, you know tha only reason he sold that much is because nobody opens shop on Sunday."

"Damn nigga, stop hatin, give my young'n his props."

"I bet he wouldn't been able to do this shit tomorrow."

"Would you be willing to put ya money where ya mouth is?"

"I'll bet you 5 g's that he can't sell 2 birds or better."

"Make it 10 and you got a bet."

"Bet."

"Aye Yo Tweek, let me holla at you for a sec."

"What up big homie?"

"Check this out, Imma let you run tha block again tomorrow."

"I got tha first shift anyway."

"I mean do ya thing like you did today."

"Are you serious?"

"Yeah."

"You must really want me to get my money up."

"Truth be told Tweek, Cal said he's tired of you being broke."

"I know Cal didn't say that because of tha conversation we had yesterday."

"I heard that."

"You never know, I might blow past you."

"I doubt that young'n and since you talkin, I bet ya boss 10 g's that you couldn't dump 2 birds tomorrow, you want to bet something?"

Since I had tha whole Philly coming to cop, I knew this would be easy money.

"How much you want to bet?"

"What ever ya pockets can stand."

"I can cover anything." I looked at Cal who gave me a look that said take his money.

"Bet 50."

"Nigga I ain't betting no 50 dollars! 50 stacks."

"Do you even have that much money?"

"Ha! Ha! Ha! Ha! I should be asking you that."

"Bet and I don't want no bullshit wit my money."

"How about give it to Cal to hold so it won't be no excuses when it's time for me to get my money."

"I'll be right back." When Box left I let Cal know that I didn't mean no disrespect, but Box was try'n to play me.

"I know and you handled it tha way you were supposed to."

"I know that is ya man and that is tha only reason he's still breathing, so please talk to ya man." I knew that Tweek was telling tha truth because he was a gun and had no problem putting in work.

When I got to tha crib I took tha 60 grand out my stash leaving me wit 40.

"Damn I hope I win this bet or Imma be Fucked up. Tweek probably spending his whole stash try'n to get a double up, if it wasn't for Cal I would just take his money." I got back to tha block just as Tweek was pulling up.

"Was you able to get tha money?" I asked being petty. "I'm sure what ever you couldn't get, Cal will put up for you."

"Box you a funny dude considering that 60 is majority of ya

stash." I must have hit a nerve or been speaking tha truth because tha smile he was just wearing was replaced by a frown. So to make matters worse I said, "We can always lower tha bet if that"s too much for you to handle."

"Nigga if you built like that bet another 40 g's."

"Box I don"t want to take all ya money and leave you assed out, then you gon' have to borrow something from my boss to get back."

"Put up or shut up nigga! Go get tha last of ya stash." I really didn't want to bet my last, but I wasn't going to let this mafucka talk shit.

"I'll be right back, you just make sure you got yours."

"I made that last night. Ha! Ha! Ha!"

On tha ride to get tha last of my stash, I came to grips that I was going to be 100 grand richer, there's no way he's going to off 2 birds when tha rest of tha city is back up and running.

"Tweek, do you think you will be able to pull it off?"

"Listen Cal, tha way tha block is doing numbers, now is tha way it's going to be from now on."

"Well in that case, it's time to step up tha look outs."

"All you need to do is put 4 runners on tha roof tops, that way they'll be able to see everything from all angles."

"Tweek, should've been had ya own organization."

"Maybe I would've if I would've had a nigga like you on my side."

CHAPTER 21

Spence asked Zoey to Marry Him

"What are you doing?"

"On my way to pick Spence up from tha train station."

"Oh shit, he's coming home this weekend?"

"Yup, my Baby will be here in 45 minutes, so bye."

"Bye Bitch, call me when you finish getting ya freak on."

"And you know I will."

I got to tha train station wit 10 minutes to spare. After a couple of minutes, I saw Spence coming out tha front door. I ran to him and stuck my tongue right in his mouth. When we finally came up for air, everybody was staring at us.

"Damn it feels so good to hold you. Its been almost 4 months since you were home for Christmas break, besides I know you had plenty bitches to keep you occupied."

"Zell, you know I only have eyes for you."

"What ever, come on let's go. What would you like for dinner? Wait, wait let me guess; steak, baked potatoes, corn on tha cob, salad and garlic bread."

"If you knew why did you ask?"

"You too damn smart, I didn't miss that."

"Why you taking everything so serious, you know I'm just messing wit you."

"I need to stop at tha supermarket to grab some cucumbers and salad dressing." Gizelle had no idea how much I loved her, but she would soon find out.

"Damn Zell, that was delicious."

"Why thank you Baby, I'm glad you liked it."

"So what's for dessert?" he asked wit lust in his eyes?

"Cherry pie."

"Ummm, sounds good, I haven't had Cherry pie in months."

"Why don't you get in tha shower while I clean these dishes." By tha time I had finished tha dishes Spence was getting out of tha shower.

"That's right go get that thing nice and clean for Daddy." 30 minutes later, I was walking into tha bedroom wit my birthday suit on.

"Wow, you look like you put on a little weight."

"Oh my God, do I?"

"Yeah, but its not a bad thing, believe me," he said smacking me on my ass.

"Can you hand me my towel and nightgown please?"

"You won't be needing this," he said referring to my nightgown, but handing me tha towel. While I was drying off, Spence started rubbing my shoulders.

"That feels so good."

"Lay down so I can give you a full body massage."

I didn't say anything, I just did as I was told and let Spence massage me from head to toe. When I felt his tongue on my lower back, I knew was about to be on. Just tha thought of finally getting some made my pussy moist.

When I felt Zell's body tense up, I knew I had her so I slid my tongue down tha crack of her ass. She perched her ass in tha air so I could get under her. I slid my face where it needed to be and caressed her clit wit my tongue.

"Ooooooh Baaaaaby," tha sound of Zell moaning turned me on which made me suck harder on her clit.

"Oh my God Baby I'm about to Cum!" I used my tongue to bring her to tha brink of no return. Once she started shaking, I knew what time it was so I sucked her clit as if it were a piece candy.

"Oooooooh Baaaaaaby! IIIIII'mmm Cumming! Oooooooh Mmmmmy Goooood!" Once I had drained that first nut out of her, I turned her over so that I could make love to her. One hour and 6 orgasms later we both laid in tha bed exhausted.

"Thanks Baby, I really needed that."

"So did I, a girl needs tha real deal instead of toys." We talked for a while until we eventually fell asleep in each other arms.

When I woke up my nose was filled wit tha smell of eggs, waffles, beef bacon and turkey sausage. I walked in tha kitchen to find Zell and a pair of boy shorts and a half shirt.

"You decided to get up?"

"Yeah, why you ain't wake me up?"

"I was going to wait until breakfast was done."

"I hope you don't wear those outside."

"Pleeeeease, I wouldn't dare go outside wit these on, I might cause an accident."

"Ha! Ha! Very funny."

"Boy sit down so you can eat."

"I think I just lost my appetite."

"Oh no you didn't after I bust my butt to cook this."

"I'm sorry, but I'm not hungry." I could tell she was pissed so I let her know I was just joking.

"You play too much," she said punching me in tha arm.

"Ain't no fun when tha rabbit got tha gun."

"So what's on tha agenda for today?"

"I don't know."

"I know you want to visit ya peoples."

"We can do that later or tomorrow, today is about us."

"Well, what do you suggest we do Spence?" For starters, Spence dropped down on one knee, I thought he wanted some more Cherry pie until he pulled out a box and asked me to marry him.

"Aaaaaaa! Aaah! Oh my God! Oh my God! Is this a joke? Where is Ashton Kusher, I know I'm getting punked?" Once he opened tha box I knew it wasn't a joke.

"So will you marry me Gizelle?"

"Oh my God! Oh my God! Yes Spence, yes I will." He put that big ass diamond on my finger and I couldn't stop looking at it.

"Go head, call Zoey, I know you want to."

"I'll call her later, this calls for some celebration."

CHAPTER 22

Cookin tha Work and Watchin tha Block

"Aye yo Cal, I told you that was tha easiest 90 grand I ever made."

"You just made me 10 stacks, what do you say we hit Eagles tonight and have a few drinks?"

"I'm going to have to pass on that, I still got tha block until 12 o'clock."

"Well, we can go after that."

"That's cool."

"Listen Tweek, I'm not going to have you working a shift anymore."

"So what do you want me to do?"

"Cook tha work and watch over tha block."

"Come on Cal, ain't no money in that."

"More then you was making working a shift, especially tha way you got tha block doing major numbers."

"Cal it's all about tha product, if tha product is good, one fiend will tell another and they want that work no matter where they gotta go to get it. I normally get 46 off a bird. I get 50 easy."

"Damn and that shit still fire like that?"

"Yeah that was my best class in school, Chemistry."

"Why didn't you finish school?"

"I graduated last year wit a 4.0., Cal I'm not no dumb nigga. I do what I do, but I still went to school."

"Ya boy ain't been around yet?"

"Nah, him, Glass and KC went to dinner wit some broads. He must have told them niggaz about tha money he lost."

"Why you say that?"

"Glass had tha nerve to ask me if he could hold 5 stacks."

"You'll never get ya doe back."

"I know, that's why I told him I didn't have it."

"He knew you did, that's why he asked."

"Cal it ain't no Fuckin way either of them niggaz should be broke."

"You got to figure, all they do is buy clothes and weed."

"Yeah, but why would you do that if ya money ain't right?"

"Tweek, Imma keep it real, if it wasn't for you and Box, I would never have put them on."

"We was all doing our thing, but once I saw that I was tha only one bringing in tha money, I went on my own way. I'm not gonna be tha only one hustling, but we splitting tha profits 3 ways."

"I feel you. That's my mom hold up Cal…"

(Anwersing the other line)

"Hey mom. What, When? I'm on my way."

"Yo, I gotta handle something urgent, can you hold me down for about a half?"

"Yeah, go handle ya biz." I knew it was something important, so I had no problem holding tha block down.

"Mom are you a'ight?"

"Yes, we just got here. Tha only thing that was tore up was tha kitchen, basement, and my bedroom."

"Mom call tha locksmith and have tha looks changed. Also tomorrow have an alarm put in." I reached in my pocket and handed her ten 100 dollar bills.

"Tweek, it's not going to cost that much."

"What ever is left spend on you and Dasia."

"Tweek you don't have any ideal who might have done this?"

"No mom, but I'll find out."

"Do you want me to call tha police?"

"No!" I left and headed back to tha block.

"Good lookin' Cal I appreciate that."

"No problem, is everything cool?"

"Somebody broke in my mom's house."

"Did they get anything?"

"Hell no, I don't even live there, I got my own spot. So why would they go there? Nobody knows I don't live there, tha funny thing is they only ram shackled tha three spots where I kept my money and coke." I looked at Cal, but before I could say anything Glass, KC and Box pulled up.

"I'll talk to you after they leave."

"Damn little nigga, you still around? I thought you'd be out celebrating."

"Celebrating what?"

"All that money you just won."

"I would of but somebody broke in my crib and took it." I peeped how they all looked at one another.

"Was ya mom or Dasia there?"

"No."

"You don't know who did it?"

"Nah."

"And you said they took that 90 g's huh?"

"Yeah it ain't bout nothing, it was free."

"Box I though yall had some broads lined up for tonight?"

"We did, but they backed out at the last minute."

"Glass I need you to take the first shift."

"Tweek has tha first shift."

"Not any more, I moved up in tha world."

"Cal, what tha Fuck he talkin bout?"

"From now on Tweek will be cookin tha work.

"Nigga that ain't moving up, that's down grading." Ha! Ha! Ha! They all started laughing.

"He'll also be watching over tha block."

"Damn, why yall stop laughing?"

"Cal how you gonna give this nigga that type pull."

"Why? Because I got tha block doing 216 grand a day easy."

"Cal you ready to get those drinks?"

"You still got an hour left."

"Imma let my peeps have it for tha last hour."

"You got some work for us?"

"Yeah, how much yall got to spend?"

They both looked at me like sad puppies.

"I only got a stack on me."

"Yeah me too."

"I got 2 ounces for that."

"2 ounces nigga, we pose to be family."

"I know, you getting at a few ones and you letting that shit go to ya head.”

“I ain't lettin shit go to my head, I'm just not lookin out for nobody that ain't try'n to come up.”

“So what tha Fuck you sayin?”

“Look, lets keep it 100, yall don't want to stack no paper cause if you did, yall would be up by now. Plus I'm pretty sure Box got yall covered. Cal said yall his young'ins.”

I didn't say shit to Cal, but I think Box is broke too.

“Cal let me holla at you for a sec.”

“What's up Box?”

“I need a favor.”

“I'm listening.”

“I need you to hold something.”

“I know you ain't broke.”

“That was my last I lost.”

“How was that ya last, you ain't been stackin?”

“Nah.”

“No wonder ya young'ins is Fucked up, they following ya lead.”

“I guess that sayin is true, ‘Don't blame tha young'ins, blame tha old heads for not showing them tha proper guidance.”

“Why would you bet that 100 grand if you knew it was all you had?”

“I couldn't let that nigga play me, plus I thought it was a sure win.”

“Box you gonna have to earn ya keeps like everybody else.”

“I know you not going to play me like that Cal.”

“You played ya self, Box you should be sittin on at least a quarter mil, if not more.”

"Shit happens."

"Yeah and you just happen to be broke so you better work this shift."

"What?"

"You heard me."

"Fuck that, I ain't none of these young mafuckas!" What ever they were talkin bout was pretty intense, but it was none of my biz-ness so I kept pitching.

Cal walked back over, "Lets roll Tweek." If looks could kill I would be dead tha way them niggaz is lookin at me.

For a Monday it was packed at Eagles. We grabbed two stools at tha bar and ordered some drinks.

"Tweek, let me tell you somethin."

"You know I'm always game for knowledge."

"Tha minute you start really getting paper you see who really is down wit you. A mother finds herself always try'n to protect her child, but once he grows up, he's on his own. Don't get it twisted she still has his best interest, but he's old enough to make his own decisions."

"Cal cut through tha bullshit and just say what you mean."

"Yeah you're right I am rambling. How tha Fuck can Box be broke?"

"Oh shit! I Fuckin knew it. Cal I knew that nigga was broke, just like tha ones that hit my crib."

"How you know that?"

"Did you see tha way they looked when I said they took that money and then tha way Box said so they got that 90g's."

"Funny you say that cause I thought it was just me, but I did notice it."

"Glass and KC were tha only ones that knew about those spots. I only said they took that money so they would wonder which one of them got tha doe."

"Smart thinkin."

"Once I find out for sure they going straight to tha boneyard, ya boy Box included."

"Tweek if that nigga had anything to do wit it, Fuck 'em 'Death B-4 Dishonor!'"

"He had tha nerve to get mad cause I told him he gotta work shifts to get back Ha! Ha! Ha!"

"Word? You told him that?"

"Mafuckin right! He got to get it from tha muscle like we do, ain't nobody ever give me shit."

"'Wheeeew' Shorty bad as a mafucka!"

"Who her?"

"Yeah."

"Man that's Zoey."

"You know her Cal?"

"Yup that's my son's aunt."

"Say Word."

"Word."

"Damn she bad."

"Relax, she too old for you."

"How old is she?"

"24 or 25."

"Man and that's only a couple years."

"Stay in ya lane little nigga."

"Oh shit, here she comes, how I look?"

"Ha! Ha! Ha! Hey Cal."

"What up Zoey?"

"Shit just came to have a few drinks, can I sit wit yall?"

"Sure, what you drinkin?"

"Bombay and Cranberry."

I had to laugh at Tweek when he started coughing. "Oh my bag… Zoey, this my boy Tweek."

"Hey Tweek."

"What's up angel?"

"Boy didn't he just say my name was Zoey?"

"My fault, you just look like you dropped outta Heaven."

"That was cute, thanks for tha compliment."

We sat, drank and talked for another hour, tha whole time Tweek was spittin his game. I had to admit he had Zoey smiling and blushing.

"Well, I'm bout to get up outta here, I'll see yall later."

"I hope so," Tweek said wit a smile.

After she left I asked why he didn't ask for her number.

"Never ask a female for her number, if she want you to have it, she'll give it to you."

"Well I guess she didn't want you to have it."

"Nah, she just gonna ask about me and once she finds out I'm straight, she'll call you."

"You got it all figured out huh?"

"I hope I do."

"Tha average chicken head would have gave tha number and pussy up, but Zoey has class."

"Tweek, you had her laughing and blushing, I haven't seen her like that in a long time."

"Any man would be lucky to call her his wifey."

"Her fiancé was killed about 8 months ago."

"I didn't know, if did, I would have fell back."

"You remember Quez?"

"King of Philly Quez?"

"Yeah, that was her fiancé."

"Seriously."

"Yeah seriously."

"Damn, then she's caked up, I'm glad I didn't come at her like no nigga wit a lot of doe."

"You played it just like you suppose to."

"Cal, I can't front, I'm feeling Zoey like a mafucka.

CHAPTER 23

Zoey and Tweek Become Friends

While I was in tha shower, I couldn't help, but think about Tweek. Even though he was young, he was sexy and he didn't try to come off like something he wasn't. Now that I think about it, he kinda reminds me of Quez, 6-1, brown skin, brown eyes and corn rows that hung to his shoulders; not to mention he has game. *"Oh my God! Oh my God! Zoey what are you saying, he's too young for you."* All I could do was smile as I thought about tha compliment he was giving me. *"I can't mess wit him, I'm 6 years his senior."* As I dried off I looked at myself in tha full body mirror that was on tha back of my bedroom door. I have put on some weight I'm going back to tha gym in tha morning; even though I picked all tha weight up in tha right places. As soon as my head touched tha pillow I was out like a light.

(Dreaming) It was you. I can't believe it but why? I thought I could trust you, you we're suppose to be family; how could you have Quez killed. Just as I was about to shoot, I woke up face drenched wit sweat.

For tha past month, I've been havin tha same dream, waking up at tha same part. There has to be some truth to this dream, if only I can stay sleep long enough to see who this person is. I looked at tha clock on my nightstand, since it was 6 o' clock, I got up to take a shower so I could go to tha gym.

I pulled into tha parking lot and noticed there were a lot of cars there already. I grabbed my gym bag in my iPod then headed in. Since it was my first day back in a few months, I decided I would only work on tha treadmill, stairstepper, and do some crunchies. I was about 15 minutes into my workout when I noticed a familiar face walk in, of course I acted as if I didn't see him. When I was about to get on tha treadmill, Tweek walked over to me and asked if he could go for a jog wit me? I thought that was cute, so how could I say no.

"So do you come here often?"

"Every day, this ya first day?"

"Nah, I actually have been coming here for years, I just haven't been in tha past 2 months."

"I wanted to apologize for last night."

"For what?"

"Cal told me that you lost ya fiancé and I didn't..."

I put up my hand cutting him off, "No need to apologize you did nothing wrong. Actually, I haven't laughed like that in months."

"Zoey can I be totally honest wit you?"

"Honesty is always tha best policy."

"I know that you're not lookin for a relationship and thats all good, but everybody could use a friend."

"So what are you getting at?"

"I just want to be ya friend if possible and before you say it, age is just a number."

"Now you sound like Aaliyah."

"Comedian I see."

"Ha! Ha! Ha! I'm just joking," I said looking at his chiseled frame.

"We can be friends; would like to have my number?"

"Certainly."

"How come you didn't ask last night?"

"You're never pose to ask a lady for her number, if she wants you to have it, she'll give it to you, after she does a background check that is."

"Boy you crazy, but right," I said wit a smile.

"All you have to do is ask me and I'll tell you."

"Well in that case..."

"Hold up, not now."

"How about over lunch at Ms. Tootsies?"

"That's my favorite spot."

"Mines too, that's why I suggested it."

"Well if nothing else, we have that in common."

He turned me on to a nice calisthenic workout that had me tired as shit when we were done.

"Do you come in tha mornings every day?"

"Yes, unless I have something to do."

"Well, I guess I have a new workout partner."

"I guess you do."

"Oh shit!"

"Whats wrong?"

"I have an appointment in 45 minutes to get my wig done," he said pointing to his ponytail.

"Who does it?"

"My peeps Lisa at Zoacis."

"I heard of that place."

"Yeah, I can't front, its nice as shit, whoever designed it has class."

"Thank you."

"Excuse me."

"I said thank you."

"I know, but for what?"

"Saying I have class."

"Oh shit, tha Zo is for Zoey?"

"You're cute, funny and smart."

"Yeah, you can say that."

"If you don't mind me asking what made you open up a salon?"

"My little cousin always had my auntie house crowded wit her customers doing hair."

"So you basically open tha shop for her?"

"Yup thats why its called Zoacis."

"Acis is ya cuz?"

"Yeah, you know her?"

"She use to holla at my peeps."

"Umm Hmm...I bet."

"Ask her."

"I'm not going through all that," I said knowing damn well I was."

Once we finished working out I decided to go home and shower instead of doing it at tha gym like I usually did.

"Zoey would it be OK if we did dinner instead?"

"Sure that will be fine, I have to go to tha shop and do some paperwork anyway."

"I'll see you there."

"Probably not, I'll be in my office."

"Do you like Japanese?"

"Yes."

"There's a new Japanese spot that just opened up, we can go there."

"Wherever you want to go it's a'ight wit me, here's my number." We exchanged numbers before getting into our cars.

It was 12 o'clock by tha time I got to tha shop.

"Hey Zoey."

"What's good Acis?" Tha shop was always packed no matter what day it was.

"Acis, when you get a minute come holla at me."

"A'ight." I looked over to Lisa's station to see if Tweek was over there, but he wasn't. I had just hung up tha phone wit my mom when Acis walked in.

"What's wrong wit ya hands?"

She looked down then said, "Nothing."

"Must be since you just walked in wit out knocking."

"Well excuuuuse me," she said walking back out.

(Knock, Knock) "Come in."

"Is that better?"

"Much. So what's on ya mind favorite cousin of mine?"

"I need some info on somebody."

"Hold up." She opened tha door and told Tasha to prep her next client then sat down.

"I'm all ears."

"I bet you are, but seriously do you know Tweek?"

"Sexy ass Tweek from 52nd?"

"Yeah, sure do."

"What's up wit him?"

"On what type time, biz-ness or personal?"

"Both."

"Ooooooh, let me find out you feeling tha young'in."

"Nah, he was wit Cal last night when I went to tha bar."

"Well, he use to talk to one of my girls until he found out she was in his pockets."

"So he got money?" I asked not really caring if he did or didnt.

"I guess, she didn't want for nothing. She didn't even like him."

"Why not?"

"Because she was siked for some nigga who was doggin her and not doing a damn thing for her."

"So how did they stop seeing each other?"

"I told him what she was doing. And no, I don't like him, I mess wit his cousin."

"Sean cousin?"

"Yup. Now don't get it twisted, he's one of tha good ones."

A big smile spread across my face.

"What are you smiling about?" Acis asked as she turned to look.

"Let me find out you're really feeling Tweek."

"Well let me get out of here and get some hair done."

"I'll talk to you later, I'm about to take my mom to lunch."

"Bitch you just want to walk past Tweek, uh oh Stella try'n to get her groove back."

"Shut up! Acis, you make it seem like I'm old; I'm only 24."

"I know and Tweek is 18, get ya couger on."

"I might be mistaken, but you and Sean is about 5 years apart."

"No bitch 4."

"Don't you have a birthday coming up?"

"OK…OK, I get tha point. Besides he is very mature for his age. Call me when you and Aunt Zelda finish."

I stayed in tha office for a few more minutes to make sure I had everything we needed ordered. As I was leaving tha office my mom called to say that she forgot she had a board meeting and wouldn't be able to do lunch. So I called Zell who said she was just about to grab a bite to eat.

"Zoey where are you and Aunt Zelda going to lunch?"

"She canceled, so me and Zell are going to Minato's in Wilmington."

"You going all tha way to Wilmington for lunch?"

"Girl they got tha best Shrimp Fried Rice I ever tasted."

"Zoey you not lying, I ate from there a couple times wit my friend from Wilmington," Shay one of tha stylist said.

"Well can you get me a platter?" Acis asked handing me 20.

"A'ight."

"Me too?" Shay asked.

"I got tha phone number, you might as well order now that way by tha time you get there it'll be done."

"What's tha number?" I ordered, then walked out of tha shop but not before smiling at Tweek.

"Hello."

"You didn't ask me if I wanted anything."

"I'm sorry, but I figured you would be gone by tha time I got back."

"I probably will be, but that doesn't mean that you couldn't bring it to me."

"You're right, would you like something?"

"Thanks, but no thank you."

"Imma hurt you going through all that for nothing."

"It wasn't for nothing, it was an excuse to call."

"You don't need an excuse to call."

"Wow, I'm flattered, I really am."

"Boy you crazy. We still on for dinner, right? Unless you choose to take one of ya other friends."

"I guess that means yes since I don't have no other friends."

"I hear you, I'll call you around 8 o'clock."

"I'll be waiting on that call."

CHAPTER 24

Tha Plan

"A'ight which one of you mafuckas got that scratch?"

"I was about to ask tha same question."

"Yeah me too."

"Somebody got tha paper."

"We all left together, so where would any of us have put that money?"

"You know what I think?"

"What's that KC?"

"Tweek didn't want any of us to ask for no change, so he made that shit up. Now that I think about it we haven't left each other side since we went in there."

"That nigga is a sucker. So if he's not keeping his money in his crib, where tha Fuck is he keeping it?"

"Cal probably got it put up for him."

"Fuck Cal!"

"Yeah, was up wit you earlier?"

"That nigga is starting to think his shit don't stink. Do you know that nigga had tha audacity to tell me he wants me to start working shifts?"

"Nah, he ain't try'n to son you like that."

"Tha Fuck if he didn't, we need to rob his ass."

"Not a bad ideal, but there's only one problem."

"What's that?"

"I'm tha only one who knows where his Ducky Spot is."

"Do you think he keeps any money where he lays his head at? I got a better plan, but one of us is going to have to get shot."

"I don't like tha sound of this already," Glass said.

"Hold up young'n, let's hear him out."

"So what's tha plan KC?"

"Listen, we already know Cal is going to bring a few bricks thru."

"Keep going."

"After we knock that shift off, two of us will mask up and run in Ms. Wilma's and come out wit tha loot."

"Sounds like a winner, so who's getting shot?"

"I will," Box said wit out thinking about it."

"It will look more believable if I get hit plus he said he wants me to work shifts."

"Next question, leg or arm?"

"I'll take a leg shot, just make sure you don't hit an artery." We went over tha plan for tha next few days and decided we will do it Saturday, since that's when we made tha most money."

CHAPTER 25

Planning an End to Zoey's Reign

"I'm on my way right now. I'll be in a blue Lexus."

"I'm in a gray rental," before I could respond tha phone went dead.

Damn that was quick he must of been around tha corner. I got out to get in his car.

"What's up?"

"Same shit different smell."

"I heard that. When do you plan on putting an end to her reign?"

"Soon, and when I do, she will never know what hit her; she doesn't even see it coming."

"Are you going to be able to get tha plug?"

"If everything goes tha way I want to go I should, but if he doesn't bite, he'll end up like his son."

"Me and Rosco got ya back!"

"I know you do, that's why I chose tha two of you to do this wit me."

"Here's tha money I owe you for that job." I took tha money counted out 5 stacks then slid tha rest back.

"Why did you give me this back?"

"I don't need it, I'm only taking this because I need to handle something that shit was free of charge."

I looked him dead in tha eyes then said, "Real niggaz do real things, don't ever forget that. I knew you was a real mafucka when we was doing our bid and you had my back." Before I got out I let him know that I would be giving him a call soon. I had left my cell in tha car, so when I got back in it was ringing off tha chain.

"Hello."

"Damn…I been hittin ya phone for tha last 20 minutes."

"My fault, I was hollering at kin folk."

"We need to re-up, shit is getting low."

"A'ight, let me make tha call, I'll hit ya phone in a few."

"Make sure you do, my folk from Maryland called said they would be headed this way around quarter after 8 for pies."

"What's left?"

"5."

"Put that to tha side for them just in case he's not ready yet."

"Gotcha." As soon as I hung up I called Jibbs.

"Speak to me."

"You got $10 I can borrow?"

"Yeah, you need it now?"

"Yes."

"Can you come get it?"

"Where you at?"

"I just pulled up to my house."

"I'm on my way."

I knew that he was talkin about tha Stash House I always met him at so I picked tha money up and headed that way. Once everything was done I called Rosco to let him know we were up and running.

"Good cause between Chester and Delaware we need 8."

"Shit, I only grabbed 10."

"Well, you better call for another 10."

"A'ight, I'll hit you in a sec."

"Yo everything was straight, wasn't it?"

"No doubt, I just need another 10."

"Damn Baby, you ain't playing no games, I'm still here."

"On my way."

My young boys from down Wilmington was selling weight so they were running through work like Carl Lewis at a track meet.

"LT if you want I'll throw you an extra 10 every time you cop 10."

"At what price?"

"50 grand."

"Let me say this, and I say this wit no disrespect intended."

"I'm listening."

"That's all I make for myself off what I buy so all I would be doing is selling them for free, thanks but no thanks."

"I respect ya honesty and hopefully tha price will drop for both of us real soon."

"I hope so, I'll be in touch." On my way to tha Stash House I called Rosco so he could meet me and we could handle biz-ness.

CHAPTER 26

Tweek and Zoey Goes Out

"Hey are we still on for dinner?"

"Yup, I was just about to call you."

"Oh were you?"

"Yes I was, smart ass."

"I wasn't try'n to be smart."

"Where you at so I can come scoop you?"

"I'm driving."

"Excuse me, Ms. too Cute to be in my Bonneville."

"Do you have a Navi system?"

"No."

"OK then."

"You don't know how to get to tha restaurant?"

"If I knew that we would be going in ya car."

"I'm at my crib in Upper Darby."

"Upper Darby?"

"Yes."

"Where at?"

After he gave me tha address I just smiled.

"How long will it take you to get here?"

"Not long."

"Do you want me to talk to you until you get here?"

"That's up to you, I'm out front."

"How did you get here so fast?"

"You won't believe me if I told you."

"Try me."

"I live around tha corner."

"Are you seriously telling me that you live around tha corner from me."

"When you told me where you live I couldn't believe it myself."

"What was tha chances of that?"

"I know…right."

"So who you live wit, ya mom or ya girl?"

"I already told you I don't have no girl and I live by myself."

"If you don't mind me asking, what made you move out here?"

"I didn't want to sleep where I shit at, if you understand that." I punched in tha address and let tha Navi take us to our destination.

"I hope I didn't have to get all dressed up?"

"Un, uh, you look fine." And he did wit his pink Ralph Lauren capris, white Ralph Lauren shirt and sneaks wit no socks.

"Lisa hooked ya wig up I see."

"Yeah, she make sure I'm straight every week."

When we got out to go in tha restaurant Tweek complimented me on how I looked. I had on my peach Michael Kors dress that complemented every curve.

Damn she bad as a mafucka, I'm not going to let her get away from me. We got to tha door only to be told we had to remove our shoes. I started to say something then I remembered that it was what they did in Japan. Tha hostess led us to our table that was stationed around a stove wit pillows for us to sit on. When tha waiter handed us tha menu he said something in Japanese to my surprise Zoey responded back.

"You speak Japanese?"

"Yeah, a little."

"Wow, is there anything you can't do?"

After we ordered our food, we talked and as it turned out, we had a lot in common.

"Just so you know Zoey, I'm not try'n to have sex wit you."

"Just so you know, you don't have to worry about having sex wit me. Now that we have that cleared up let me ask you a question.."

"Shoot."

"Why don't you have a girl?"

"Truthfully, I can't find a real woman who's looking for a commitment, they all want one thing…"

"Money?" we both said in unison.

"I'm not stingy, but when that's all they want, I'm no fool."

"From tha looks of it I would think that you were a playa."

"Unh, unh, nah, that's never been my style, I have a little sister and I would never want anybody to dog her."

"This food is delicious. Do you like to go out?"

"I really don't go out much."

"That's right, you're not 21 yet."

"That's not why, I do have a fake ID. Would you like to go to tha movies?"

"To see what?"

"Precious."

"Is that tha movie wit Monique?"

"Yeah, her and Mariah."

"I wanted to check that out anyway. We can go tomorrow if that's cool, tonight we can hit Samba and have a few drinks."

"You're driving."

"Well let's bounce."

"Check please."

"I got it."

"Yeah right, Zoey ain't no way Imma let you pay for dinner."

"And why not?"

"What kinda man lets a woman pay for dinner on tha first date anyway?"

"Ha! Ha! Ha! Boy you are funny. Do you mind driving, I'm stuffed?"

"Sure," I said after catching tha keys as she tossed them over tha hood.

As I put my seatbelt on I couldn't help but to laugh.

"Oh hey, I never drove anything nice like this." I respected his honesty and even though I'm not ready for relationship I definitely could see myself wit Tweek.

"Is it always this packed?"

"Not like this, must be something going on tonight."

"You want to go somewhere else?"

"Nah, we good, unless you want to find a parking spot." We finally found a spot a few blocks away.

"I'm not waiting in this long ass line."

"We don't have to," I said pointing to tha side door where people were paying extra to get in. When we got to tha door it cost us $50 a piece to get in.

"Why is it so packed tonight?"

"Because Gilly, Meek Millz and Young Chris is performing."

"Do yall have VIP?"

"Yeah, but that will be another 100."

"A piece?"

"No, total." Tweek paid him tha buck and he put tha bands on us. As soon as we got in we went straight to tha bar.

"First round on me, what you drinking?"

"Remy straight."

"Is that Zoey over there at tha bar?"

"Yeah, and who is that sexy mafucka she wit?"

"Hey Cuz."

"Hey Mya, Shanelle."

"What brings you out tonight?"

"Last time I checked I was grown."

"You so damn smart, so who's ya friend?"

"Tweek this is my cousin Mya and her friend Shanelle."

"How are you ladies doing?"

"Fine, but even better if you buy us a drink."

"Mya!"

"Its cool Zoey, what yall drinking?"

"Remy." Tweek pulled out a 20 and handed it to Mya.

"What's this for?"

"For ya drinks," I said letting her know she better take it before she ends up wit nothing.

"Come on, let's head to VIP."

"I'm sorry about that, she always on some other shit."

"It ain't bout nuffin, if you didn't say she was ya folk, I would've never known."

"Yeah, she is so embarrassing, I swear she is."

"What she eat don't make you shit."

"I know, but she's family and I value family."

"I had a ball, I haven't had this much fun in a long time."

"I'm glad you enjoyed ya self." Tweek pulled up to his house and woke me up. I must have dozed off.

"You said you live around tha corner."

"Yeah. I'm going to drive you home and walk back."

"You don't have to do that."

"I insist, now which way am I going?"

"Straight, when you get to tha corner make a left, then drive to tha middle of tha block."

"Wow, you literally live around tha corner."

"I told you. Pull in tha driveway. So we on for tomorrow right?"

"Yup, I'll check tha times then call you to see what time is best for you."

"When you call just let me know what time tha movie starts."

"Tweek, you don't have to compensate me."

"You heard what I said, have a good night and I'll see you later."

I walked in my front door all smiles, he was so much like Quez. I think Quez sent him to me, as crazy as that sounds. I couldn't fall asleep so I just laid there wit thoughts of my movie date wit Tweek later today. Imma just ride this thing out and see where it goes.

I couldn't get Zoey outta of my head. I've never liked a female as much as I liked her. I made up my mind that I would have her in my life. I know that she is feeling me as well because she ask me to go to tha movies wit her. I'm not going to rush into anything because I know that she's still deeply hurt behind tha loss of Quez, but I do want to see her happy. I made a mental note to call Cal in tha morning to thank him for introducing us. I put that picture of me and Zoey on tha nightstand then dozed off wondering if I was congesting her mind as she was mines.

I woke up wit a big smile on my face as I remember tha events of tha previous night. I can't believe I'm acting like this over a young boy. As I was taking tha things outta my bag, I pulled out tha picture me and Tweek took last night. Even I had to admit we did look good together and he looked much older then his 18 years. I needed to call Zell to fill her in on tha last night events.

"Hello."

"Hey how's tha engaged doing this morning?"

"Fine, I just got off tha phone wit Spence."

"How is he?"

"Nervous about tha draft in 3 weeks."

"Is he going to Memphis still?"

"He said he'll probably go second to tha Knicks, because Memphis needs a center."

"Oh so they gonna grab Roy Hollis from Wake Forest?"

"Yup, that's what it looks like."

"Is Spence mad that he won't be tha first overall pick?"

"Not at all, he said he rather play for tha Knicks since that's his favorite team."

"Mines too, especially since he'll be playing for us maybe we'll make tha playoffs finally."

"Oh yeah, I forgot you was a die hard Knicks too."

"You will be too once Spence gets drafted."

"I'm a Laker fan for life."

"Enough about that, tell me about ya date wit young'n."

"We went to that Japanese restaurant, tha food is off tha wall like Michael Jackson."

"Bitch you stupid."

"Seriously, you have to go there. After dinner we went to Samba's."

"How did he get in there tha way they be carding?"

"Fake ID. Tell me why Mya was there."

"Oh God."

"Of course she asked Tweek to buy her and Shanelle a drink."

"I'm not surprised."

"When he gave her a dub she had tha nerve to ask him what she was posed to do wit that."

"I told her she better be happy wit that. A Bitch ain't never grateful."

"So you had a good time?"

"Girl I needed that."

"You deserve it."

"We going to see Precious tonight."

"So you really feeling him huh?"

"Truthfully Zell, he reminds me of Quez in a lot of ways."

"Does he know that you do what you do?"

"Nah, I didn't tell him about none of that, if it gets serious then I'll let him know."

"So where is he coppin his work at?"

"He's Cal's young boy."

"Does Cal know that his work comes from you?"

"Nope."

"Well, if you ask me, I think you need to tell Cal and sell him tha shit at ya number cause I know Jibbs is taxin him."

"I thought about that before Tweek even came into tha picture."

"You know Jibbs is going to be upset."

"So what Zoey, if it wasn't for you he'd still be struggling."

"True, but he is family. He'd do it to you if he could."

"A'ight, let me call him and Cal."

"Ok, make sure you call me later."

"I will, love you Cuz."

"Love you too."

Once I was finished getting dressed I decided to go by tha shop to see if Acis could do my hair. I walked into tha shop to be stopped by a dozen roses that sat at tha front desk.

"I see somebody put it down last night. Yeah, you must have because these are for you."

"For me?"

"Yes, for you," Acis said wit a big smile.

"I don't know why you smiling."

"They said you would say that."

"What ever, do you have time to bump my hair?"

"Sure, I could squeeze you in for nice tip."

"I have a tip for you, start turning tha alarm on at night when you leave." Ha! Ha! Ha! Tha whole shop was laughing.

"Ha, ha very funny."

"No seriously, start turning tha alarm on when you leave or who ever is tha last one to leave."

I picked up tha card that was attached to tha roses.

Hey you, just wanted to say thanks for tha good time last night, can't wait to see you tonight. Ya friend, you know who.

"You really like him huh?"

I turned around to face Acis, "He's really nice."

"Come on so I can bump ya hair for ya date."

"Who said I had a date?"

"Come on Zoey it's me you talking to."

"We're only going to tha movies."

"Zoey, you have been through so much pain these past 8 months, you deserve to be happy."

"Do I?"

"It's what Quez would have wanted. You will always carry him in ya heart and you should, but you can't put ya life on hold forever." I didn't say anything, I just listened to Acis talk cause deep down I knew what she was say'n was tha truth, I just was not or am not ready to say goodbye to Quez,

"Zoey, Zoey."

"Huh."

"Did you hear anything I just said?"

"Yeah, I heard you."

"Well, think about what I said."

"I will."

"Now get out of my chair so I can make some money."

"Here," I said handing her 40 dollars."

"What's that for?"

"I pay just like everybody else."

"In that case, you owe me another dub." I went into my bag to give her tha other 20.

"If you don't put that back in ya purse."

"Let me get outta of here, I have to pick Calry up."

"Where is he?"

"Home, but I promise to take him to Chuck E Cheese's today."

"He called me this morning and asked me if he could stay tha night."

"Here Chuck E Cheese's is on me."

"Where is Lad?"

"Home wit my mom. Imma stop by there and pick him up."

"You want me to call?"

"Please, and tell Aunt Masiah to have him ready cause you know how she is."

"Don't I know."

CHAPTER 27

Tweek and Zoey Coincidentally Meet

I decided to take my flowers home where I could keep them alive for a few days. I still couldn't believe Tweek went through tha trouble of sending me flowers. By tha time I picked up Calry and Lad it was 2 o'clock.

"Where do yall want to go?"

"Chuck E Cheese's!" tha both yelled.

"Aunty can we eat pizza and play games?"

"You sure can."

"Welcome to Chuck E Cheese's."

"Can we have a table in tha back please?"

"Yes and what kind of pizza?"

Before she could finish Calry yelled, "Pepperoni!"

"2 large Pepperoni and a pitcher of fruit punch." I paid for everything then followed her to our table.

On tha way to tha table I thought I saw Tweek going to tha restroom. That's a shame, I have him on my mind that much that I'm thinking he's actually at Chuck E Cheese's.

"Wow! You wouldn't be following me, now would you?" I looked up wit a mouth full of pizza surprised to see Tweek.

"What are you doing here?" He pointed at this pretty little girl running past.

"You didn't say you had a daughter."

"Because I don't, that's my little sister."

"Wow, she can pass for ya daughter."

"Everybody says that, so what brings you here?"

"See those two little boys playing wit ya sister."

"Oh shit, ain't that Cal's son?"

"Yup and my nephew."

"He did say his fiancé was ya sister."

"Are you going to just stand there or are you going to join me?"

"I don't want to intrude."

"You won't, besides it looks like they're having fun."

"Thank you."

"For what?"

"Tha beautiful roses you sent."

"Oh that was just to show you I appreciated last night."

"You could have just said that instead of going through all that trouble."

"Zoey, believe me, it was no trouble at all."

Before we knew it, it was close to 8 o'clock and tha kids were not even considering leaving.

"What times does tha movie start?"

"8 o'clock, but we can always catch tha 12 o'clock movie at Painters Crossing."

"A'ight cause by tha looks of it we gonna be here for at least another hour. Might as well get some more tokens and order another pizza."

CHAPTER 28

Box Works tha Block

"So you gonna work tha block tonight?"

"Do I have a choice?"

"Not if you wanna make some money." I couldn't wait to pull tha shit off tonight to bring this nigga back to reality.

"Me and Ciara are going to Atlantic City for tha night, so Imma leave enough shit to hold you down." *This is gonna work out better than I thought.*

"Box you really need to stack ya paper because ain't no way you shouldn't be worth at least 5 or 6 figures by now."

"Hey man, like I said shit happens."

I looked at him to see if I could detect if he was back Fuckin wit that dope, but didn't see any indications that he was.

"Why you lookin at me like that?"

"I just can't believe you're broke, that's all."

"I won't be for long," I thought to myself causing me to smile. "Well, I need to handle some last minute shit before I go, so I'll hit you up later."

He won't be talkin that money grip shit after tonight. "Ha! Ha! Ha!"

"What's so funny?"

"Just thinkin about tonight. It's definitely on."

"Yeah, Cal just told me he'll be outta town until tomorrow, so he's gonna probably hit us heavy."

"I got 4 words to say, 'Show me tha money!'"

"I already called Glass so he could meet us here."

"That nigga would be late to his own funeral."

"Who you telling."

After leaving Box I decided to hit Tweek.

"What up big homey?

"Damn, where you at, a birthday party?"

"Nah, I brought my little sister to Chuck E Cheese's."

"You wouldn't happen to be wit Zoey, would you?

"Why would you ask that?"

"For starters, I know she was suppose to take my son there today."

"She's here, but it was coincidental, nothing planned."

"Yeah yeah."

"Seriously, we have a date later."

"So you really feeling her huh?"

"I told you that tha first time I saw her."

"I was calling to let you know I will be outta town until late tomorrow."

"Biz-ness."

"No me and tha Misses going to AC."

"You need me to hold tha block down?"

"Nah, you enjoy ya date, I got Box handling that.

"Don't lose too much money, I would hate to have to put you back on."

"Nigga I ain't no fool. I do want you to pick up tha money when you finish ya date."

"No problem, gotcha big homey."

"I'll holla at you when I touch down and tell my sis-in-law hi."

"Will do."

As soon as I hung up I called Jibbs to grab 5 birds, I figured that should be more than enough to hold them down til I get back.

"Cal you might as well just bring money for 2 since I owe you 3."

"Oh shit, I forgot about that."

"I didn't."

"I'm on my way, same restaurant?"

"Yes." When I got there Jibbs was already waiting on me.

"Yo, did Zoey get at you yet?"

"Nah, why, what's up?"

"Nothing, she wanted to talk to you. You really forgot about tha 3 bricks I owed you?"

"Yeah, I been so busy getting my money right."

"Yeah, you definitely been getting ya money right, you started wit 4½, now you at 15 bricks."

"When you got a mafucka whose wit you, then you can't help but to stack up."

"I feel you, but let me get on my way, I got another stop to make."

I couldn't help but wonder what Zoey wanted to holla at me about, so I hit her her phone.

"Hello."

"Zoey, I just left Jibbs and he said you needed to holla at me."

"I do, but let me hit you back when I leave here."

"I'll be at tha house and don't be long cause we need to drop Calry off at ya moms."

"Why don't yall just meet me at moms in an hour?"

"A'ight."

"Ms. Wilma have you seen Box?"

"He went to get some more bags."

"When he comes back give him this, let him know its 3 and if he needs more give him this."

"Do you want me to put this up?"

"Yes, it's 2 in there, if he doesn't need it then just hold on to it."

"Are you going some where?"

"Yeah, but I'll be back tomorrow and Tweek will be by later to pick up tha money."

"Aunty, can Lad stay tha night?"

"You have to ask ya mom-mom and his mom."

"Can you call them please?" I dialed my moms number first, then my aunts.

"Lad staying tha night...yup, yup Lad staying tha night."

"I'm staying tha night! I'm staying tha night!" All I could do was laugh when I look in tha mirror and saw them dancing.

"Aunty, Aunt Masiah said she would bring Lad's clothes by."

We pulled up tha same time and Cal and Ciara where there.

"Mommy! Daddy!" Calry yelled once he saw them.

"Did yall have fun?"

"Yes and we spent all aunty's money, thats why we had to leave so early."

"Early, yall were there for 7 hours. Come on so yall can get a bath."

"So what's up Zoey?"

"Cal this doesn't go past us."

"You can trust me Zoey."

"I know you been getting ya work for 30 a bird from Jibbs."

"I don't owe him no money. In fact, he just paid me tha 3 birds he owed me."

"Hold on, I didn't say you did, what I'm saying is you're paying too much."

Cal had a confused look on his face.

"From this point on, you'll be dealing wit me at a price of 25 a bird."

"Huh?"

"You heard me nigga."

"Zoey, Jibbs put me on when I didn't have shit, he even gave me a brick for free."

"Nigga where you think that shit came from? Who you think put him on? Where you think he getting his work, Me nigga me!"

"Oh shit, how long have you been in tha game?"

"That's not important, I was tired of Ciara complaining about bills and other shit, so I put you in position where you could come up and you did."

"Does Tweek know?"

"No and I'd like to keep it that way."

"Zoey, my young boy is really feeling you and I don't want him to get hurt."

"I appreciate ya concern Cal, but me and Tweek are just friends and he knows it."

"Friends? For now anyway."

"Is Tweek getting money like that?"

"He's doing his thing."

"Well, you make sure you give it to him for tha same number you getting them for."

"Zoey, so you mean to tell me that bird came from you?"

"Yup, I wanted to see if you had it in you or if you were just in tha way."

"Well, I guess you found out a nigga just needed some help."

"So when we get back in town I'll hit ya phone, Imma need 15."

"Wow, only a few months and you doing 15."

"I'm not playing no games."

"I see."

"Ms. Wilma did Cal drop that off?"

"Yes, it's here."

"Can you get everything ready for me while I use tha bathroom?"

"There is a such word as please!"

"Don't worry about it, I'll get it myself."

I'm bout sick of this old Bitch wit her smart ass mouth, I got something for her. I made a phone call while I was in tha bathroom so she wouldn't be in my biz-ness. Glass came in while I was cooking tha work.

"You need some help?"

"No but you can help bag that shit up."

"You talk to KC?"

"Just hung up wit him."

For tha next 2 hours I cooked while they bagged tha coke.

"Box Imma get wit you tomorrow, I got a hot date tonight."

"Nigga we got work to do."

"I been try'n to hit Shanty for a minute now I'm not passing this up."

"What tha Fuck is up wit you and KC?"

"Ain't shit up wit me. Must be you, putting Bitches over money!"

Tha money was flowing non-stop. I looked at my watch and it was close to 2 am, so I went into Ms. Wilma's to wait on Glass and KC.

"Cal said Tweek would be by to pick tha money up."

"What?"

"Tweek's coming by to pick tha money up."

"When?"

"He didn't say, he just said he would be by after his date."

CHAPTER 29

Where is tha Money and tha Drugs?

BOOM! "Everybody get tha Fuck Down Now!"

"Yo what tha Fuck is going on?"

"Nigga if you don't get tha Fuck Down they gonna be cleaning up ya brains off tha wall. Now where tha Fuck is tha money and drugs!"

"I don't know what you talking about."

SMACK! "Mafucka play dumb if you want."

"Yo grab that Bitch over there!"

"Where tha doe at Bitch?"

"I don't know."

SMACK! "Aaaaahh!!!" Blood came down her face.

POP! "Oh shit, this Mafucka shot me."

"This my last time asking where is tha money at?"

"Ms. Wilma tell 'em where it is."

When she didn't say shit, I told them where it was. Once they got tha doe and tha rest of tha coke, they ran out.

"Ms. Wilma I need you to take me to tha hospital now!" She went upstairs wit out a care in tha world.

"Did you hear what I said?" After about 5 minutes she came back down stairs wit her head bandaged up.

"Where are ya keys? We taking ya car."

"You not getting in my car wit all that blood, either give me ya keys or stay there and bleed to death." I should have told them to shoot her in tha head instead of pistol whipping her.

"Here," I said throwing her my keys.

"Now help me to tha car."

"You better help ya damn self."

"This old Bitch just earned a one way ticket to tha bone yard."

By tha time we got to tha hospital I had lost a lot of blood. Tha last thing I remember was being put on tha stretcher. When I came to, Glass in KC were staring at me wit smiles on their faces.

"We thought we gonna lose you."

"Yeah, tha doctor said another 10 minutes and we would have been making funeral arrangements."

"That dumb ass old Bitch, she act like she didn't want to bring me to tha hospital."

"I told you to let me put one in her head."

"Ha! Ha! Ha!"

"What's so funny nigga?"

"If you didn't say shit, she wasn't going to tell us where tha money was."

"I know, she would have died for that shit."

"I guess she'd rather die than to tell where that doe was. Tha doctor said you can go home in a couple days."

"A couple of days, man I ain't try'n to be here that long. I need to call Cal."

"We already did."

"What he say?"

"He was on his way, Ms. Wilma had already called him."

"I bet she did."

"Cal said that she sustained a concussion, but she'll be fine."

"Did yall put everything up?"

"Yeah, we got 60 a piece and you got 80."

"Damn that's all?"

"Yeah and about half a pie."

"Listen, I risk my life for this shit, so Imma take a hundred grand and 9 ounces."

"I'm cool wit it."

"Yeah you got that? Listen, also don't go spending that money or selling that shit, we got to be smart about this."

"Yo you a'ight?" Cal asked walking in.

"Yeah, I've been better."

"From tha looks of it, Imma have to agree wit you on that."

"So what happen? And why tha Fuck were you two not there?"

"I had some pussy lined up."

"Me too."

"Pussy? You mean to tell me that Pussy is more important than money? I see why you niggaz is Fuckin broke!"

"Cal, I told them to take tha night off."

"Why tha Fuck would you do that wit out having somebody to watch ya back? If you had those look outs on tha roof, none of this shit wouldn't have happen."

"Oh so now this is my fault?"

"I'm just say'n."

"What tha Fuck are you say'n?"

"I'm tha one shot in tha hospital! And I'm tha one out 120 grand! Nigga you come in here acting all concern when all you really care about is ya

Fuckin money. Fuck you nigga!”

"That medicine is Fuckin wit ya mind.”

"Nah, I just see who you really are and you can step.”

"You right, I don't need you nigga you need me! Wit out me or my boys you'll have to play tha block you and ya flunky.”

"It doesn't matter and just so you know, my flunky as you call him, has more money than you will ever have.”

I took a mental note of that then said, "As of this moment I don't exist to you.”

This nigga gon' have tha nerve to say that we can't hustle on tha block. He gon' find his ass up in one of these beds or tha bone yard. Nah, I would never send him to tha bone yard, unless he takes me there.

CHAPTER 30

Tweek and Zoey Spends Quality Time

"That was a real emotional movie. I normally don't watch movies like that, but it was good."

"Its ok to go outside tha box some times."

"What's that suppose to mean? You watch movies that deal wit drugs, sex and murder, right?"

"I understand now."

"Do you read?"

"Yes."

"Who is ya favorite author?"

"I like tha boy Jerz."

"Boy shut up, I love his books. I'm reading 'No Loyalty' right now."

"Oh yeah, that was real good, especially tha part..."

"Ssssh, don't tell me."

"My fault, you gonna love it though. I'm reading, *'What You Don't Know Can Hurt You.'*"

"Now that is tha shit! He's up and coming."

"Yeah and he's from Wilmington."

"Do you want to go get something eat from Dennys?"

"Sure, I just need to make a call first."

"Make it on tha way."

"No problem."

Voicemail answers: Hello you have reached Wilma please leave a message. "She's probably sleep, let me hit KC or Glass. Yo, are you on tha block?"

"Nah."

"Is Glass out there?"

"Nah he just left, why what's up?"

"I need to tell Box that I will be by to pick that money up in about an hour."

"I'll hit his phone and let him know."

"Bet, good lookin; is every thing straight?"

"Yeah, I just had to pick up some money for Cal."

"So what you hustle for Cal?"

"Yes and no."

"I'm not following you."

"It's like this, Cal helped a nigga get right, once I did, he let me have tha block on Sunday since we didn't pump on that day. Long story short, I ended up making a lot of doe."

"I know Box not feeling that, he's a jealous nigga."

"I know."

"He tried to get at me when Quez was alive, but he's not my type and I don't trust him."

"Yeah, I think he had something to do wit my moms house being broken into."

"Are you serious?"

"Yup."

I explained tha story to her and full.

"So ya own boys did some shit like that to you?"

"Zoey them niggaz ain't my boys and they never have been, but one thing for sure, two things for certain, when I find out for sure they're outta here; all three of 'em."

"You haven't even touched ya food."

"I wasn't really hungry."

"Then why did you come?"

"Just to spend more time wit you honestly."

"You didn't have to do that."

"At 2 in tha morning what was I going to say, hey let's go back to my place to talk."

"Yes."

"Yeah a'ight."

"No seriously, that wouldn't have been a bad idea."

"I'll try that next time."

"You like plays?"

"I never been to a play before."

"Well, I have two tickets to see Why Men Cheat, if you're interested."

"When is tha play?"

"Tomorrow evening."

"Well I must be one lucky dude."

"Why is that?"

"Three dates in a row what a beautiful lady."

"I don't believe in luck."

"You believe that everything happens for a reason?"

"Yes, I do."

On tha way home I asked Tweek if he could change one thing in his life what would it be.

"Zoey, I have to be honest I would never have gotten into tha game."

"A lot of hustlers say that."

"I don't plan to do this for tha rest of my life."

"Nobody does, but when you make a lot of money is hard to just walk away from it."

"I know and that's why you have to start some legit shit that generates good money."

"That doesn't always happen."

"True, but it's definitely worth a shot."

From that moment I knew that despite his age he had a head on his shoulders.

"You seem like you have it all thought out."

"Not really, I just know I don't want to be 30 years old still in tha game."

"I feel you on that and I did cause, I planned on getting out in another year letting Jibbs have this shit."

I pulled up in front of Tweek's house and to my surprise he invited me in for a nightcap.

"I guess I could come in for a few, all I was going to do was play a little Xbox anyway."

"Oh you Fuck wit tha Xbox?"

"Yeah I play NBA 2K, Live Madden, all that shit."

"What you know about them games?"

"You got Xbox?"

"Fo sho."

"Well I'll show you."

We went in, but before we started I asked him to turn to Sports Center so I could see if my Knicks won.

"I can't believe this."

"What's that?"

"A woman who not only plays Xbox, but one who likes sports and has tha same basketball team as me."

"You're a Knickerbocker?"

"Die hard, even though we ain't done shit since we went to tha finals that lock out season in 99."

"Yup tha Spurs put it on us."

"Don't remind me."

"We'll be a'ight next year after tha draft."

"Yeah, we posed to grab up Spence."

"Yup that's my cousin's fiancé."

"Word…Spence is my cousin."

"Ya pretend or real cousins?"

"Real…my mom and his mom are sisters. I'll be there wit him on draft day along wit my mom, aunt and Zell."

"Oh shit, I kept say'n I seen you some where before, but it was Zell. yall look alike but her hair is shorter."

"I know I hear that all tha time when we were growing up, a lot of people thought we were twins."

"Damn we beat Labron and Shaq."

"I know…turn tha game on so I can bust that ass."

"Ha! Ha! Ha! We'll see."

"I'm running wit tha Celtics."

"I run wit Kobe."

It was a close game until tha last 3 minutes of tha 4th Quarter, I had to take over wit Kobe.

"You played a good game."

"What ever run it back."

We did wit tha same results.

"Put in Madden."

"A'ight."

She picked tha Colts, I grabbed tha Packers. I couldn't front, her Madden game was on point; she bust my ass 3 straight times.

"You might can beat me in live but I own you in this."

"I better get my ass home, I got a lot of things to do today."

"On a Sunday?"

"Yeah."

"I have an ideal."

"What's that?"

"What time is tha play?"

"9 o'clock."

"Would you like to go to dinner first?

"Sure, where we going?"

"What do you have a taste for?"

"Steak and shrimp."

"Fried or steamed?"

"Either."

"I got tha perfect spot."

"Well, I'll pick you up at 6."

"I'll be waiting," I said walking her to tha front door.

CHAPTER 31

Tha Hit at Ms. Wilma's House

Zoey didn't know it, but I was cooking her dinner and since it was 6 in tha morning, I decided to get 2 hours of sleep, so I thought anyway.

Tha constant ringing of my phone woke me up out of my sleep.

"Hello," I said groggy.

"Yo a mafucka hit Ms. Wilma's spot and shot Box."

"What?"

"I don't wanna talk over tha phone, so meet me at Uncle Ducky's."

"A'ight, I'm on my way."

Uncle Ducky was code word for Ducky's Spot.

"So were did Box get shot?"

"In his leg."

"How much paper did they get?"

"I hit 'em wit 3 bricks, so what ever they made off of that."

"Look Cal Imma pay you for tha three bricks since it was my fault."

"How was it ya fault?"

"If I wasn't so wrapped up wit Zoey, I would have been able to slide thru and pick that doe up."

"Tweek this shit ain't ya fault, if I was wit they bad ass chick, I would've done tha same shit. If Glass and KC was out there, maybe this shit wouldn't have happened!"

"Is Ms. Wilma OK?"

"Yeah, she just got a concussion from being hit wit a pistol."

"What time did this happen?"

"Ms Wilma said about 2."

"That explains why she didn't answer her phone when I called."

"But when I called KC he said that Glass was out there, but he just left."

"Is Box a'ight?"

"Yeah he is fine, he said it was my fault since we never put anybody on tha rooftops."

"You said Box only got shot in tha leg."

"Yeah that's right."

I didn't say anything, but I had a feeling Box, KC and Glass were behind it.

"So I guess Box will be out of commission for a while?"

"Fuck that nigga!"

"Huh?"

"That mafucka had tha nerve to say that me and my flunky will have to work tha block wit out him and his young'ins."

"So I'm a flunky now?"

"I checked him and I also told them they can't pump on tha block no more."

"I know they didn't like that too much."

"Tweek I don't give a Fuck what they like, it's a done deal! So until we get another team, me and you will handle tha block."

"No problem, just one thing."

"What is that?"

"I want to go in wit you on tha work."

"Done."

"Just like that?"

"Just like that. I have a few people who will be more than happy to work for us not to mention they're loyal and trustworthy."

"Sounds like you were already starting to assemble a team."

"Yeah I was gonna let you know, I wasn't just gonna bail out on you."

"Well I got four niggaz for tha rooftops already."

"Ride wit me over to West Philly."

"Why what's up?"

"No sense in waiting, we might as well get this up and running today."

"Well my folks just dropped tha numbers yesterday to 25 stacks."

"Damn thats a good number."

"I know, I normally do 15 but now Imma do 20."

"I can match that."

"Damn you holdin like that?"

"Cal I'm bout this money."

"Tweek we bout to take this shit to a whole nother level."

"I got a date tonight wit Zoey, but Imma let her know I can't make it."

"No, no, no, you go on that date, I'll take care of shit tonight."

"Good lookin Cuz Imma cook her dinner tonight."

"Wow, you really feeling her."

"Yeah, females like her don't come around too often."

"I know, I got her sister."

2½ hours later everything was set in motion, funny thing is 2 of tha 5 niggaz were my cousins; talk about small world. After everything was straight I had to hit tha supermarket so I could get what I needed for dinner. I also let Cal know that sooner or later he would have to introduce me to tha Connect, just in case he was ever out of town and we needed to score. He said he would talk to tha Connect today to see if it was cool.

"What's up Cal?"

"Hey little Sis." I filled her in on tha situation wit Box.

"Cal you know I'm not one to sugar coat shit, but I think Box and those other two Cats did this."

"You said it was two robbers and Box only got hit in tha leg."

"Yeah."

"Well, do tha math."

I had to admit it did sound suspicious after Zoey broke it down.

"Zoey I swear, if that nigga betrayed me like that, he's a dead man walking."

"Me and Tweek decided to become partners so Imma need 40." Tha look on her face said it all.

"Yeah, I told him I was going to grab 20 and he matched it, I didn't even see he was holding like that. He thinks it's best that I introduce him to tha plug so if I'm not around he can still handle biz-ness."

"That's a good ideal, I'll do it tonight over dinner."

"Zoey, ya biz-ness is ya biz-ness, but it seems you like him just as much as he does you."

"You're right, my biz-ness is my biz-ness, so mind yours."

"My fault! Damn."

"Nah, I'm just playin wit you, I can't front, he reminds me of Quez in a lot of ways and we have so much in common."

"Ciara said that she hasn't seen you this happy since Quez was alive."

"Despite tha 6 year age difference, he is very mature and smart. We had a serious talk a few weeks ago that's when I discovered how intelligent he was."

"Cal, I'll be honest, me and Tweek have a good time together, but I'm not ready to jump into a relationship yet because I don't want to be hurt. I let Tweek know that and he understands, so its no pressure on either of us."

"Hey all yall can do is go wit tha flow and let tha chips fall where they may. Well, enjoy ya date tonight and I'll get wit you tomorrow."

When I got in tha house I wasted no time prepping tha food. I wonder if I should grill tha steak or put it in tha oven. After some thought I decided to put it in my George Foreman Grill. Zoey called to say she was on her way to pick me up. I still needed a few more minutes for tha salad I was making. When she said she was out front, I told her to come in.

"You know tha play starts at nine."

"I know, just come in." *"He must want some, get back in Madden," I thought to myself.*

"It smells good in here."

I decided to cook dinner instead of going out to eat.

"Can you cook?"

"I burns in tha kitchen."

"Well, I'll be tha judge of that."

"Now I don't want you to go crazy once you taste my cookin."

"Don't flatter ya self."

"You'll see."

"What did you cook anyway?"

"Steak, steamed and fried shrimp, baked potatoes, corn on tha cob wit a salad."

Wow, you cooked all of that?"

"It wasn't bout nothin."

"Let me wash my hands, where's tha bathroom at?"

"Down tha hall, second door on tha left."

I couldn't believe Tweek went through all this trouble, I was really impressed, I just hope he could cook.

"What kind of dressing would you like for ya salad?"

"Do you have Blue Cheese and Italian?"

"Sure do."

"This salad looks really tasty."

"I made it from scratch."

"You went through all of this for me?"

"I love to cook, especially for other people."

"I must admit this salad taste like something from Saladworks."

"Wait until you taste tha main course then," I said bringing her a plate.

"Aren't you going to eat something?"

"I'm just going to eat some salad, I'll eat later." I figured now was a good time to talk to him about biz-ness.

"Umm, mmm mmn, you wasn't lying boy, you can cook ya ass off."

"So does that mean you like it."

"That would be an understatement, everything is seasoned perfectly."

"So Cal tells me you want to meet tha Connect."

"Huh," I said.

"Nah I heard what you said, but why would he tell you that?"

"Simple, I'm tha Connect."

"Hold on, hold on, hold up, you mean to tell me you're..."

"Yes, I am," I said cutting him off before he could finish his sentence.

"I would never have thought."

"I know and that's tha way it's suppose to be."

"Hold up let me get this right, this whole time you been tha one supplying tha city?"

"Pretty much."

"Impressed but not surprised."

"And why is that?

"I'm just not, you're a strong black women. I don't know if I'm going to be able to date my Connect."

"Why not?"

"That's was pose' to be a joke."

"Oh my bag! Ha! Ha! Ha!"

I said mustering up a fake laugh.

"Zoey, you too much."

"So I've been told."

"Nah, seriously, can I ask you a question?"

"Anything."

"What made you wanna get in this game?"

"I just didn't want to see what Quez built go to somebody that didn't deserve it."

"Not that you don't already know, but this game is full of sharks."

"I do know and its OK, I'm tha Queen shark, my bite hurts too, ask Joey." I didn't say shit, I just looked at her and nodded.

"Damn, Zoey was definitely about her biz-ness, I had heard about that shit wit Joey from Cal."

"I never liked his bitch ass anyway," I said breaking tha silence.

After I put tha plates in tha dishwasher and tha food away, we made our way to tha theater.

CHAPTER 32

Draft Day

This was tha day we had all been waiting for, Draft Day. I couldn't help but smile when I looked over at Tweek and Zoey, they have been really kickin it strong these past few months, but what really made me smile was Spence sitting there playing wit his napkin.

"Nervous?"

"Huh?"

"You nervous?"

"How you know?"

I pointed to his napkin. "It's OK to be nervous," his mom said.

"Yeah nigga, just don't fall when you go up there."

"Tweek that's not nice," Tweek's mom said.

"Mom I'm just joking."

Tha Lottery finally got underway. Wit tha number 1 pick tha Memphis, Grizzlies pick Roy Hollis from Wake Forest. Everybody applauded. His mom and dad went crazy, I could tell he was a little embarrassed.

"Please don't do that to me."

"Boy shut up," Zell said.

Wit tha number 2 pick tha New York Knicks pick Spencer King from North Carolina. So not to embarrass Spence, we all just applauded loudly. Spence walked up to tha podium, shook David Stern's hand then put his Knicks Fitted on while holding his jersey up for everybody to see. Once tha draft was over we all went out to dinner to celebrate.

Spencer got his first taste of stardom when some guy walked up and said, "Spence I'm glad we got you in New York, I've been following you since high school."

"That's whats up, I just hope I can help tha team."

"I know you will, I think you were clearly tha number 1 pick, but hey Memphis lost our gain. I'm going to let you get back to ya meal, but before I do could I have ya autograph?"

"Sure."

"This will be worth a lot of money in tha future."

"Damn Big Man, if you thought you were dreaming, you know now," Tweek said hi fiving Spence.

"Baby you made it."

"Yes I did mom and I'm going to buy you and Aunt Josslynn nice big house."

"Boy you will do no such thing, I love my house."

"Me too."

I had to smile, Tweek and Spence's mom were twins and even though they were in their late fifties they did not look a day over thirty five.

"You just make sure you put my daughter-in-law and a big ol' house."

"He doesn't have to do that Mom Ross."

"Oh yes he does," Tweek mom added.

"So did you guys set a date yet?"

"Sometime next summer."

After dinner we decided to finish celebrating by going out to party while Ms. Josslynn and Ms. Rosslynn went back to tha hotel. I couldn't believe how many people were coming up to Spence and he hadn't even put on a Knicks uniform yet.

One dude walked up to Spence and said, "Yo Imma tell my uncle to get you some help."

We later found out that his uncle owned tha Knicks. Spence wasn't a drinker, but tonight he was throwing Bombay back like water.

"We better get him back to tha hotel before he passes out."

Since me and Tweek weren't ready to leave we decided to stay and had Spence catch a cab back to tha hotel. Despite all tha fine women in tha club, Zoey was by far tha baddest chick in tha building, judging by all tha stares. I wasn't tha only one who thought so either. One guy even had tha nerve to offer to buy her a drink.

"I don't think my man would approve of that."

"My bag son, no disrespect intended."

"None taken."

"I like tha sound of that."

"Sound of what?"

"You know, when you said ya man."

"Oh you do huh?"

"Sure do, but I'm not in no rush, it'll happen sooner or later."

He was probably right and at this rate, sooner than later.

CHAPTER 33

Taking It to tha Next Level

"Jibbs we need to get at Zoey, we at tha bottom of tha barrel."

"She's outta town, she won't be back til tomorrow."

"Fuck! I don't think we got enough to hold us down til then."

"You never got wit tha Plug did you?"

"Fuck no!"

"You flaggin a nigga?"

"Man its not my shit."

"How we pose to make a move wit out tha Plug?"

"Nigga we gon' be good, Imma let her know when she gets back, we need to do something."

"Yeah cause we can't be ass out when she decides to just up and leave town."

"It could be just my shit and if I'm outta line let me know, but she act like she don't want you to meet tha Plug."

"I think that's his shit, he's a scared nigga."

"What tha Fuck that nigga scared of?"

"Man that's how niggaz be when they getting serious paper like that, they don't wanna meet nobody new."

"Jibbs, I understand all that, but you Zoey's cousin, not to mention we tha ones moving all tha Fuckin work."

"Bo just be patient, we gon' get our turn wit or wit out tha Connect, I promise."

"Jibbs don't get my wrong, I definitely appreciate what she did for us, but damn, don't stop us from taking it to tha next level."

"If nothing else you should know I will never let anyone stop me from moving up, not even family."

"So we just going to let them have tha block like that huh?"

"Of course not, but we're not in position to go to war wit them niggaz, not yet anyway."

"So what do you suggest we do?"

"Get on tha grind and stop bullshit'n for starters."

"Easier said than done."

"Why is that?"

"That means no clubbing, no weed, no clothes, and no Bitches."

"Well if yall wanna keep doing all that, go ahead, but I'm bout to get my money up."

"I have a better idea."

"I'm listening."

"Fuck tha fast way, lets get this shit tha ski mask way!"

Tha light went on in my head. "Yo, why don't we just rob niggaz?"

"Man Box wasn't you paying attention? I just said that."

"I know this store in Allentown where we can get tha stuff we need."

"What are we still standing here for then?"

"Shit, I'm waiting on yall."

When we arrived at tha store all I could say was, "KC you a Fuckin genius."

"I've been told that a few times before."

We got everything we needed and headed back home.

"I know this Cat in Pottstown that's eating."

"A'ight he'll be our first victim."

"Do you know tha layout?"

"We can scout it out for a few days."

"A few days? Is tha pay off gonna be worth it?"

"Of course, I'm not doing no petty robberys, 5 or 6 figures. If I take a risk its gonna be worth it."

"I"m wit you on that KC," said pulling out his 40 Cal wit a big smile on his face.

For tha next few days we got tha nigga Kanes routine down to a science. Every detail from tha time he goes to sleep to even reading Playboy when he takes a shit.

"Yall ready to do this shit?"

"I was born ready."

"Me too, lets make it happen."

"On three 1, 2, 3 BOOM!

"FBI every body down now!"

Tha 3 guys that were in tha house hit tha floor so fast I had to stop myself from laughing. KC put tha plastic handcuffs on them while we searched tha house.

"We got 30 minutes before they get here, so let's find this paper."

We split up so we could find it quicker. As I was tearing up one of tha rooms I stumbled across tha floor safe.

"Oh shit," I said running back to tha other room to get tha keys I saw on tha nightstand. That was smart to put tha keys in a different room cause tha average nigga would've never figured that out. When I opened tha safe there were a lot of neat piles of money stacked in there.

"Glass said, "Lets go! I got it."

"So do I! Now help me put this into tha bag."

We got outta there wit 10 minutes to spare.

"We don't need to hit that other spot."

"Nigga we ain't doing no half ass job just cause that spot was holding."

"You right, I seen all that money we took out tha safe."

"Now remember we only have about 15 to 20 minutes tops before they arrive so in and out leave tha van runnin."

BOOM! "Every body down now! Every body down!"

Both men complied wit out any problems. This job was easier, tha money was already in duffel bags, but I still wanted to make sure that we didn't leave shit behind so I ran upstairs.

"Well, Well, Well if it isn't my friend Mr. Floor Safe."

This time there was some money and drugs, I put everything in tha bag and headed back downstairs and out tha door.

"Wheew that was easier than ordering a pizza. I could get use to this line of work real fast."

Once we got back to our Ducky Spot we wasted no time counting tha money and drugs. 3 hours later every thing was counted and divided 3 ways leaving us wit 300 grand, 3½ bricks, and a pound of weed a piece.

"Fuck hustlin, this is my new hustle! I be Fuckin wit this female in

Delaware and I remember her talkin to one of her girls about some nigga named Hakeem that she wanted to see get robbed."

"Does tha nigga got money?"

"Tha way they were talkin I would think so."

"You need to find out."

As KC was about to say something his phone rang.

"Hey I was just talkin about you to my boys."

"Oh was you? And what were you sayin about me?"

"Nothing, just that I was going to come down and pay you a visit since I haven't seen you in a minute."

"Yeah I bet."

"I was...what you doing later?"

"Me and my girls are going to this party Keem is having at tha Riverfront."

"I heard about that, it's a few fliers floating around up here not to mention they been talkin about it on tha radio."

"Why don't you and ya boys come thru?"

"You know what, we will."

"I'll hit you up a little later, I'm bout to grab me something to wear."

"Fo' real KC, don't be bullshit'n."

"Don't worry you'll see me tonight." *(They hung up tha phone and KC continues to talk to his boys.)*

"So we going to a party now?"

"Yeah tha boy Hakeem is throwing a party down there so we might as well get a jump on him and have some fun at tha same time."

"Well, let's hit King of Prussia so we can get fly."

When we pulled up to tha mall we ran into KC's old girl wit some nigga from Chester.

"What's up Balinda," I asked being petty.

"Hey Glass, Box, KC," she answered wit her nose turned up.

"You going to that party tonight in Delaware," KC asked.

"Yeah we going," she said to let us know she and dude was going together.

"Come on yall let's get this shit so we not here all night."

I knew KC had feelings for Balinda still even though he tried to deny it, so seeing her wit dude had him vexed.

"Damn KC I don't know how you let Balinda get away from you."

"It was about money wit her, she wanted more than I could give her."

"So she's a gold digger?"

"Nah, she just likes tha finer things in life which I knew from tha jump."

"So when you couldn't provide she rolled out?"

"Nah, I let her go, but I never told her why, I just said I couldn't be faithful."

"If you ask me she still wants you."

"How you figure that?"

"For starters, tha way she was acting and tha fact that she keeps looking over here at you."

I turned around to talk to see Balinda staring at me which caused me to smile at her.

"I suggest that you get her back because you're gonna have more than enough money to keep her and ya self happy. Now that we have clothes, let's grab some shades."

We walked down to tha designer frames only to run into Balinda again.

"Are you following us?" Box said wit a smile.

"Boy please."

"Excuse me can I see those Gucci frames right there please? Yo is these me?"

"Yeah."

"I'll take 'em."

"That'll be 350 dollars please."

"Can we get a deal on 3 pair of 'em?

"Let me ask my manager. I'm sorry, but she said I'm not allowed, but I'll give you my discount."

"Don't worry about it Shorty, I don't want you to get in trouble. Here you go keep tha change."

"Ooooh thank you."

"Can we get those 2 pair of Pradas please?"

"600 please." We both gave her $350 and let her keep tha change.

"If I give you my number will you call," Glass asked?

"You'll have to give it to me and find out."

It was 7 o'clock by tha time we left tha mall.

"Yo I decided I'm not poppin no more Perks (Percocets), I'm only smokin weed from here on out."

"KC I'm wit you on that and I'm only Fuckin wit E's when I go out."

"We need to start getting dress, its 8:30."

"Let me hit my cousin and see if he gonna still let me push tha six."

Once we all were dressed, we headed to my cousins house to get his car.

"Damn you niggaz try'n to get all tha bitches tonight."

I had to admit Glass and Box was killing 'em wit that Prada shit on. Don't get it twisted, I was definitely looking tha part in my Gucci.

"Wow, I know I'm knockin something down tonight, you see all tha honeys in that line?"

We pulled up to VIP, got out wit all eyes on us.

"They ain't playin no games out here, look at 'em. So this is how they do in Delaware?"

"You must be from outta town," some fat to death bad ass Chick said.

"We from Philly Ma."

"Oooooh tha big P-H-I-L-L-Y," she said singing and spelling it out.

"Tika you don't need no more to drink, Shay make sure she stays clear of tha bar."

"Damn Mommy drunk already? Yall haven't even made it inside yet."

"Don't get it Fucked up, I still know what's going on."

"We not tha ones you got to worry about. Hopefully, we'll see yall inside," Glass said as we walked to tha VIP line.

"First round on yall," one of them yelled.

"Fo' sho, Ma Fo' sho."

"Aye yo Keem, this party is serious."

"I know and there still a whole bunch of people try'n to get in."

"Yo let's go take a couple pictures."

"Hey Keem."

"What up Talia?"

"Yo that's tha nigga right there."

While we were taking pictures, Balinda came in wit tha same dude from earlier.

"I'm not surprised to see yall in tha picture booth."

"Take a few pictures wit us, if its a'ight wit ya peoples."

I was glad I had these shades on so she couldn't see me staring at her, cause that Gucci dress wasn't doing her body any justice.

"Balinda you look real nice."

"Thank You KC you're looking sharp ya self. I know I can get one of those pictures?"

"You sure can," Box said handing her one where she was next to me.

"Thanks," she said putting it in her handbag then walking away.

"Nigga you better tell her how you feel before it's too late."

"I thought you were bullshit'n about coming."

I turned around to find Felicia standing there in this flawless Christian Dior strapless dress.

"Damn who's this Diva?"

"Box, Glass, this is Felicia."

Don't get me wrong Balinda was bad, but she didn't have shit on Felicia.

"Where's Jazz and Rona?"

"They went to get a drink."

"I could use a drink myself."

We met up wit them at tha bar and I wasn't surprised at how good they looked after seeing Felicia. We were all formally introduced.

"Hey you said first round on you."

"No you said it, we just agreed on it."

"Well what ever, can we just get our drinks."

"Unh, unh, unh some things never change," Felicia said looking at Tika.

"Stop hatin."

"You wish I was."

Box peeled off a crisp hundred. "Enjoy tha drinks," he said handing Tika tha money.

"Thank you, come on yall."

"Aaaaahh she makes me sick," Felicia said.

"You know her?"

"Unfortunately yes, that's my sister."

"No wonder yall resemble."

"Same dad."

For tha next few hours we sat and drank wit Felicia, Jazz, and Rona.

"Do yall know that chick?" We all turned to look.

"She's been staring all night."

"She's from our neighborhood."

"That explains it, you might want to let her know yall in good hands like Allstate. Ha! Ha! Ha!" We all started laugh'n.

By tha end of tha night Jazz, Rona, Glass, and Box were very acquainted. They wanted to get a room, but I just couldn't get my mind off Balinda for some reason.

"Where yall parked at?"

"VIP."

"We'll pull around and yall can follow us."

"Cool."

On tha way to tha car Balinda and her friend rode pass. And before I knew what was going on, I blew her a kiss which caused her to smile.

"I knew he still had feelings for me," Belinda thought to herself.

As they rode past KC he blew her a kiss; at that moment she made up her mind that she will call him tomorrow and let him know how she truly felt; little did she know KC was thinking tha same exact thing at that very moment.

"What tha Fuck do you mean someone hit both Fuckin houses? How much did they get? I want to know who tha Fuck did this! As soon as you hear anything I want you to give me a call, but in tha meantime biz-ness as usual. Make sure you get those cameras installed and put two shooters in each house so this doesn't happen again."

"Jibbs how much did they get?"

"900 grand, 3½ bricks, and 3 pounds of weed."

"That ain't shit, it's just tha principle that a mafucka would even try us. Jibbs nobody knew that it was us they were robbing, they thought it was Kane."

"Do you think he had something to do wit this?"

"Nah, that nigga maybe a lot of things but stupid ain't one."

"Don't worry we will find out who did this and when we do may God have mercy on them.

I know what I meant to ask, did you talk to Zoey about meeting tha plug again?"

"Yeah, she said she would holla at him and let me know something by tha end of next week."

"Now we making progress. I gotta go meet Rosco and LT, I'll hit you up later."

"A'ight."

I called LT to let him know I was on my way and what kind of car I would be in. I pulled up, got out and walked into tha corner store followed by Rosco and LT.

"Was that my cousin Jibbs that just walked in tha store?"

"Girl yeah, they need to meet somewhere else, instead of that Bodesa all tha time."

"Who's they?"

"Him, LT, and Rosco."

"Oh my God! I know he not deal'n wit them after Zoey told him not to."

"He's been dealin' wit them for a while now."

"How you know?"

"I live right here, ain't too much around here I don't know bout."

"Unh, unh, unh."

"Hey you didn't hear that from me, I don't want to get mixed up in what ever is going on."

"Riz, I would never put you in tha middle of anything, we been friends too long, you should know that by now."

"I do Zell, I do."

"Yo, have ya man go get that outta tha car so I can bounce."

"He already got it and tha money is in there, I'll hit you up when I'm ready."

"No doubt."

"What's tha deal wit that other thing? Or is it off?"

"Hell nah, we still on, it just might take a little bit longer."

"OK, as long as we still on."

"You know you'll be tha first person I call when it happens."

After Jibbs got in his car and pulled off, LT and Rosco came out, looked around, then got into their car and left also.

"Riz, how long did you say they have been meeting here."

"For tha past couple of months."

"You sure?"

"Yeah, I haven't been spy'n, but every time I go to tha store or just happen to look out my door, they're there.

"OK and thanks again Riz."

"Maybe we can get together this weekend"

"OK just call me cause this is my weekend off." As soon as I got into my car I called Zoey. *Answering machine picks up: Hey you know who you called and you know what to do so do it.*

"Hey Cuz, I got something to tell you, so soon as you get this hit me up bye."

"Oh shit," I said looking at my watch. "I'm suppose to meet wit Spence's mom for lunch to talk about tha wedding plans."

"Hello."

"Hey Ms. Rosslynn."

"Hey Honey ya on ya way?"

"Yes, I'll be there in 15 minutes."

"OK, I'll be out front waiting."

Sure enough Ms. Rosslynn was out front waiting wit her Christian Dior sun dress and matching sandals on.

HONK! HONK! "Girl I'm right here."

"Oh I thought you was one of those young girls stand'n there lookin all fly."

"I know I could pass for 20 something, but a young girl...wow Zell."

"So where do you want to go for lunch?"

"How about TGI Fridays? I have a taste for that sizzling chicken and shrimp."

"What you know about that Ms. Rosslynn?"

"Honey me and my sister eat there all tha time."

We ate and talked about tha wedding which will be next summer at tha end of tha season.

"Oh my God! I'm so full, I'm going home to take a nap."

"That doesn't sound like a bad ideal right about now. I'll cover tha check Zell."

"You will do no such thing," I said taking tha check from her.

"I'm glad Spence is marrying you, I knew you were tha one 12 years ago."

"I bet you say that to all his girlfriends," I said wit a big smile.

"Well considering he's had tha same girlfriend for tha past almost 13 years, I don't recall."

"Damn, it has been that long? I remember when we first met..."

Zell went into deep thought:

"Man girls can't play no basketball."

"Well this girl can"

"You not playing on my team."

"I don't want to be on ya sorry team."

"Me and Lucky against you and Mouse, check ball."

"Shoot for ball."

"You shoot," he said passing me tha ball.

I shot tha ball "SWOOSH" all net, check rock. Long story short, me a Mouse beat them 26-32, and from that day on we have been inseparable.

"Zell, Zell Huh?"

"You was in la la land"

"I was just thinkin' about when me and Spence first met."

"Make sure you give me a call this weekend," Ms. Rosslynn said getting outta tha car.

"I will."

"Love you Zell."

"Love you too Ms. Rosslynn."

"This is my last time telling you about calling me that, it's Mom or Mom Rosslynn understood?"

"Yes Mom Rosslynn."

"That's more like it, now remember call me this weekend."

"I will," I said before pulling off.

"Oh shit."

"What's wrong?"

"I didn't even hear my phone ringing."

"Is it on silent or vibrate?"

"Yup its on silent, let me hit Zell back and see what she wants."

After 3 rings tha answering machine picked up, "You know who you called and what to do, so do it."

"Damn Cuz, since we playing phone tag, you're it."

"Awe that was so cute."

"Boy shut up."

"Zoey I need you to know these past 4 months have been amazing."

"Tweek I have had so much fun, especially after all I've been through."

"I don't want you to think I'm try'n to take Quez's place because I know that I can't, but what I do know is if given tha chance I can make you happy."

I didn't know what to say so I just grabbed his face and kissed him.

"What was that for?"

"I'm not allowed to kiss my man?"

"Oh so I'm ya man now?"

"I can always find me somebody else if you don't want to be."

"So you got jokes right?"

"When we first met you said I was a comedian."

"Before you even think about another nigga taking my spot you better think again."

"Well I'll take that as a yes."

"Yes all day."

"Then it's official, I'm ya Wifey so let all ya other Bitches know."

"I keep forgetting you're a comedian, I don't have no other bitches."

"You better not!"

"If I did, do you think they would have let you get all of my time these past 4 months?"

"I don't know, maybe when you was suppose to be on tha block you was wit her."

"Ha! Ha! Ha! You really are a comedian, I'm gonna get you in tha Laugh House."

"Ha! Ha! Very funny."

"I'm just messin wit you."

"I know, I was doing tha same to you."

"Did Cal call you?"

"No."

"We need to re-up and this time make it 50."

"When do you need it?"

"When ever you're ready."

"Can it wait till tha morning?"

"Yeah, we have enough to hold us down til then."

"Are you on tha block tonight?"

"No, why?"

"I wanted to go to solo and have a few drinks."

"You know they having a welcome back to Philly party for AI 'Allen Iverson' there tonight."

"Nah, I didn't know."

"Well, I guess we better change clothes then."

"We good wit what we got on"

PHHT "You can keep that on, but I'm changing my clothes."

"You're not going to have me looking all crazy."

"I knew you change ya mind."

"What are you wearing?"

"Probably a Gucci or Prada dress, why?"

"No reason, just wanted to know so I could know how to come."

"Gucci in that case."

"Say no more, I'll be back in an hour tops."

One hour later I was knocking at tha door.

"Come in Tweek, I'll be right down."

"Why you have tha door unlocked and how you know it was me?"

"First of all, I knew I would still be upstairs when you came back so I unlocked tha door. Secondly this is a quiet neighborhood nobody's coming in here but if they do, they won't leave alive," I said pulling out my Cat 9.

"You can't get in wit that."

"You can if you know tha owner."

"Did I tell you how beautiful you look?"

"No you did not."

"Zoey you look beautiful." And she did wit her black Gucci dress wit matching sandals.

"You're looking quite handsome ya self."

"Why thank you." Zoey handed me her keys.

"So I guess this means I'm driving huh?"

"Yup."

We pulled up and it was J-peed.

"You might wanna call tha owner so we don't have to stand in this long ass line."

"He's already out front, I got this Boy, fallback you dealing wit a Boss."

"My bag, I forgot who I was dealing wit. Since you a Boss, first round on you."

"You said that like its a problem."

Once we parked and got to tha club tha owner got us in.

"Two VIP please," Zoey said pulling out her neatly wrapped money."

"I got it, I said pulling out my knot." After I paid we went straight straight to VIP get our drinks.

"Bombay and Orange Juice wit a twist of cranberries."

"I know what you drink."

"Excuse me."

"Excused."

"Do you know him?"

"Who?"

"Dude over there."

"Not really he's been try'n to holla, but it ain't bout shit."

"I'm not worried about that I just asked cause he keep staring that's all."

"Why don't you wave to him or something?"

"Tweek please."

"Nah I know a lot of niggaz gonna try to get at you I don't blame them."

"One thing about me is I'm not tha type of Broad that sleeps around, if I'm wit you than I'm wit you."

"Zoey I'm not tha least bit worried about that, I trust you; not to mention I know you can hold ya own."

"Excuse me, how you doin Zoey?"

"I'm good."

"So I see, can I buy you a drink?"

"That's OK, I just got this one."

"Well next one is on me."

"I don't know if you noticed, but I'm here wit my man."

"Oh my fault, in that case let me extend tha offer and buy both of yall drinks."

"Nah we good."

"A'ight, I'll see you around Zoey," he said winking before he walked off.

"Shit like that will get him hurt."

"What?"

"Winkin his eye bullshit, cause now he disrespecting me too."

"Baby don't even worry about that."

"Zoey I've been a firm believer of once you let somebody disrespect you unless you deal wit it they'll continue to do it." All I could do was smile. Tweek was so much like Quez.

"What you smiling for?"

"We're so much alike."

"So you agree wit me?"

"Yes I do, but I don't want you getting into trouble over me."

"Don't worry I'm not going to do shit."

"Thank you."

Excuse me I have to use tha men's room."

"Hurry up, I'll wait here."

No soon as Tweek went to tha bathroom Malcolm came over.

"So is that really ya man or was you just try'n to make me jealous because it worked."

"Please don't flatter ya self."

"If that is really ya man then why didn't he say or he do shit when I winked at yout?"

"Maybe he didn't see you."

"Oh he seen me, I made sure of it."

Tweek called Gunz, "Gunz I need you to come up to solo."

"Is there a problem up there?"

"Yeah, but listen close," I said as I explained what I wanted him to do.

"Say no more, oh yeah Aunt Joss called said they were having a bar-b-que next weekend."

"I know, she called me earlier."

"A'ight, let me get dressed."

"Gunz be discreet."

"Don't I always?"

"True dat, true dat."

I walked out tha bathroom to find dude all in Zoey's face. I didn't want to jump to any conclusions so I just walked up and put my arm around Zoey.

"You a'ight?"

"Why wouldn't she be?"

Zoey sensing I was about to snap defused tha situation by say'n lets go out on tha dance floor.

"Zoey ya man don't even know what he's getting himself into."

"I told you I don't really know him, besides he's always try'n to holla at me." Tha whole time we partied I kept my eyes on dude, while he kept his on Zoey.

"Let's take a few flicks then get outta here."

When we got outside there were crowds of people standing around everywhere. On tha way to tha car we heard somebody yelled, "Talk that shit now nigga!" Next thing we knew people were screaming and running wit tha crowd.

"Come on let's get outta here!"

"Somebody call an ambulance pleeeeease!"

"I wonder what happen, I didn't hear any gunshots."

"Me either."

As I was pulling off my phone went off.

"Yo."

"You don't have to worry about Ms. Nancy's dog, tha SPCA put it to sleep."

"You sure?"

"Positive."

"A'ight, I'll hit you in tha morning."

"You hungry Zoey?"

"Like a hostage."

"You wanna go to Wawa?"

"Yeah cause ain't too much open this late plus its right down tha street."

"Damn!"

"What's wrong?"

"I was hoping to beat tha crowd."

When we got inside I went straight to tha line that only had 3 people in it.

"Yo, I can't believe Malcolm got killed," tha girl in front of us said.

"I can he's always in something, you heard what that dude said before he killed him."

"I think it was tha dude he was arguing wit by tha picture booth."

"Probably was cause dude said he would see him after tha party was over." I smiled to myself knowing that my little cuz was in tha clear.

"Oh shit!"

"What's tha matter?"

"You know who Malcolm is don't you?"

"Nah, who's dat?"

"Tha one that was try'n to holla at me."

"Oh that nigga was try'n to holla?"

"Not really, he thought I was try'n to make him jealous by say'n you was my man."

"I guess he got what he had coming."

"They said he got shot, but I didn't hear no shots."

"Must have been a silencer."

"How do you know?" she asked lookin me in my eyes.

"How else do you explain gun shots wit no sound?"

"They say tha eyes are tha window to tha soul. Zoey if you want to know anything just ask me, I will never lie to you."

"Is this ya work? Yes it is."

"When did...?"

"When I went to tha bathroom," I said cutting her off.

"You so damn slick."

"Nah dude was playin me like I was a Clown, he got me Fucked up."

I didn't tell Tweek but I respected him even more now. That night Tweek stayed wit me, but nothing happen. I have to admit I was a little shocked because I thought he would try to get in my panties since he was now my man. Even though I stayed wit Zoey I didn't try to have sex wit her, I would let her be tha one to initiate sex.

CHAPTER 34

Everybody Down!

BOOM! "FBI everybody down now!"

One of tha guys tried to break for tha back door, but was met by a shotgun to tha face.

"Now I know you heard him say everybody that means you too; now get tha Fuck down!"

After we had all of them cuffed, we searched tha whole house.

"Did you find anything Glass?"

"No, you?"

"No."

"Fuck!"

"Hey hey, what's all tha fuss about," KC asked carrying two black duffel bags.

"We came up empty."

"I didn't, let's get up outta of here."

We made it back to Stash House is 35 minutes. For a second, I thought we weren't going to get shit. We didn't do our homework to come up empty.

"So what we did come up wit?"

"600 grand and 6 bricks."

"Damn that's all, I thought it would be more than that."

"I'm not complaining about it, that's 200 grand and two more than what we had."

"You right about that. See tha thing about you that caught my eye is tha same thing that makes me...

"hello," I said answering my phone.

"That must be Balinda tha way you cheesing."

"Mind ya biz-ness," I said walking in tha other room.

"Were you busy?"

"Not really and if I was I always have time for you."

"That's what ya mouth say."

"I'm dead serious."

"Since you not busy come take me to dinner."

"On my way."

"I'll get wit yall later, I gotta a dinner date, holla."

"Ever since he's been back wit Balinda he's been happy as shit."

"I know, that's what's up though. What you bout to do?"

"I'm bout to go knock this Shorty off in Mt. Airy."

"A'ight, hit me up, I'm bout to take my daughter to Toys R Us so she can get this kitchen set she's been asking for."

I ended up letting Balinda talk me into going to Olive Garden even though I didn't like their food too much.

"You mad ain't you?"

"Nah hopefully tha food is better."

"Their food is not nasty."

"You got ya opinion and I got mines."

"Let's just go somewhere else."

"We good, I'll get 3 orders of tha boneless wings."

"That's just an appetizer."

"I know, that's why I'm going to get 3 orders."

"Boy you crazy."

"I know, crazy for letting you go tha first time."

"So you got all that playa shit out of ya system?"

"Balinda I was never a playa, I just used that as an excuse."

"So then why?"

"Because my money wasn't long enough to take care of you."

"You gotta be Fuckin kidding me?"

"No and for tha past year there's not a day that goes by that I didn't think about you or us."

"KC I don't care how much money you have, I love you for you not for ya money."

"Balinda you wear nothing but tha best from clothes to jewelry."

"True, but I work for everything I got; I don't depend on nobody."

"So who was dude you was wit?"

"Ha! Ha! Ha! I was wondering when you were gonna ask about Shane."

"Well is it serious?"

"Ha! Ha! Ha! KC, Shane is my cousin from Chester, he wanted me to go to tha party wit him and offered to buy my outfit. Now I'm independent but not stupid."

"I heard that."

Tha waiter came back wit our food. I told her to bring my appetizers when she brought Balinda's food. We talked and got caught up wit each other lives as we ate.

"I want to invest in some type of biz-ness I just don't know what yet."

"If you want to do something profitable I think you should open a game room for kids."

"I guess I could open a game room and sale cheese burgers and stuff."

"If you want to I could find tha perfect spot for you to put it."

"Would you do that please?"

"Anything for my Boo Boo."

"Is that ya phone or mine?

"It's mine, hello. Hey I was just talking about you."

"I don't know how much? Let me make a few calls and hit you back." When she hung up she had this look on her face so I asked her if everything was a'ight.

"That was Shane, it's a drought and he wants me to see if I can get him some work."

"What kind of work?"

"Cocaine."

"Why is he asking you?"

"Because last time I got Sheeda's boyfriend to sell it to him, but he's in jail now."

"What he try'n to get?"

"He said he got 25 stacks to try it out."

"Don't worry, call him back and let him know you can get it for him, but it's going to cost him 30 grand."

I had about 12 bricks from tha jobs we pulled off, I just put them up for a rainy day since I didn't need tha money. She called him back and let him know she could get it for 30 and she would call when we finished our dinner.

We pulled up to her cousins' house, I put my 45 in my waist line because there were a lot of people on tha corner.

"You don't need that."

"I'm just being safe that's all." A few people spoke to Belinda when we got out of tha car. Once we got into tha house she formally introduced us.

"Yo, if this is any good, I'll grab another 4."

"Thanks that's what's up."

"Can you be consistent," he asked after dropping it into this tube and seeing it turn dark blue.

"Yeah."

"OK cause, I'm not gonna front, it'll take me about 2 weeks to dump 'em."

"So do you want me to get tha other 4?"

"Yeah, you might as well take tha money wit you on ya way back meet me at this address." He must have seen tha look on my face.

"That's my Stash House, I don't do shit here."

"Oh OK I feel you."

"I see you got ya Baby back," he said to Belinda wit a smile.

"Yup sure did and he ain't going nowhere this time." All I could do was smile because she was right, I wasn't going anywhere.

"Thank you."

"For what?"

"Turning ya cousin on to me."

"You don't have to thank me; money for you means money for me, I mean us."

"You crazy."

"I'm just kidding."

"It's true though."

"You need to open up a bank account."

"Already got one."

"Well, I hope you putting money into it for a rainy day."

"Of course I am and I was putting $2500 and it every day for tha past 40 days."

"Ooooooh, Aaaaaah, Yeeeeees! Don't stop Glass! Don't stop!" I was try'n to wear her out and she knew it cause she was definitely throwing it back. After 15 more minutes we both collapsed on tha bed out of breath.

"Whew…I needed that. Boy you sure know how to help a Sista out when her plumbing is clogged up."

"Hey, I do what I can."

"Well in that case, can you hook a Sista up again?" she said spreading her legs wide open.

"Why certainly."

"Janeen do you have enough stuff?"

"Yes Daddy, we can go to tha counter now." While we were in line this bad ass chick came up to us and asked where we got tha Baby So Real. "You have to ask her," I said pointing to Janeen.

"Hi there cutie, where can I get one of those dolls?"

"Daddy I can show her?"

"Hold on, excuse me, I'm going to leave this here for a minute. I'll be right back so please don't send it back."

"OK sweetie," tha cashier said.

Janeen was walking fast, we had to almost run to keep up wit her. "Let me take a guess ya daughter has been asking you for one of these too?"

"No my niece, I don't have any kids."

"Lucky you, they are expensive."

"So is my niece."

"If you don't mind me asking how old is she?"

"Seven."

"Same age as me Daddy."

I paid for all tha stuff Janeen had picked out which came to almost 600 dollars.

"I see she has you wrapped around her little finger."

"Daddy's little girl you know how that goes. By tha way my name is Box."

"Shay," she said holding her hand out.

"I know I just met you, but would I be outta line asking if you'd like to go out some time? If you don't have a man of course."

"No I don't have a man and no you wouldn't be out of line."

"Well in that case, how about dinner tomorrow night?"

"I'm available, my number is 543.0424."

"I give you a call tomorrow."

"You make sure you do that Box."

"Oh I will you can count on that."

I watched as she walked to her car, ass bouncing. I know he's watching so let me give him something to look at.

Before she got into her car she turned and waved. Me and Janeen both waved back.

"Daddy I think Ms. Shay likesyou."

"Ha! Ha! Ha! You too much."

I dropped Janeen off wit tha promise to pick her up in tha morning so we could spend tha day together which she was more than happy about.

CHAPTER 35

Jibbs Lies to Zoey and tha Betrayal Starts

"Who is it?"

"Girl come open tha door."

"Well, well, well…look what tha wind blew in."

"Ha! Ha! Ha! Very funny."

"We've been playing phone tag for tha past week."

"I know between tha salon and Tweek, I've been extremely busy."

"Yeah and wit all this wedding stuff so have I, by tha way you're my Maid of Honor."

"I better be."

"Enough about that, you know Jibbs been dealing wit LT and Roscoe?"

"No he hasn't."

"Yes he has, I was over Riz house and I saw them go into tha bodega."

"That don't mean shit."

"Riz said that I needed to tell Jibbs to switch his spot up because if she knew what was going on…so did everybody else."

"I told that mafucka not to deal wit them."

I pulled my phone out and dialed his number.

"What tha biz is Cuzzo?"

"Jibbs I know you not Fuckin wit LT after I told you not to?"

"What?"

"You heard exactly what I said."

"I ain't Fuckin wit him, who told you that?"

I looked at Zell who mouthed tha words, "He's lying."

"You sure?"

"Listen I'm not, but even if I was I'ma grown ass man, I can deal wit whoever I want to deal wit."

"You know what?"

"What," he said sounding pissed.

"You right…you can and since you choose to deal wit him then you need to find another supplier!"

"What are you try'n to say?"

"I'm not try'n to say shit, I said it!"

I hung up wit out giving him tha chance to respond.

"I can't believe that mafucka."

"What did he say?"

"That he wasn't dealing wit him, but if he was, he's grown."

"No he didn't?"

"Yes tha Fuck he did, so you will have to find another plug cause I ain't giving him shit."

"Zell for tha past 3 weeks he's been on some I run this shit, type time."

"That money is going to go to his head."

"Truth be told, Cal and Tweek are bringing in tha bulk of tha money."

"I guess all Cal needed was a push."

"To think I was about to turn everything over to Jibbs."

"You getting out already?"

"I was thinking about it."

"Well if Jibbs don't get his shit together, you can always turn tha reigns over to Cal and Tweek; you'll be in a win win situation."

"Jibbs is family, but if he can't go by tha rules then hey."

"Why would he go against what I said and still dealing wit them?"

"I know, it's not like he needs tha money."

"Man that Bitch lost her Fuckin mind!"

"Who? Zoey."

"She's still not try'n to turn you on to tha plug?"

"Fuck tha plug, she had tha nerve to say that since I was dealing wit LT she was cutting me off."

"Cutting you off as in no more coke cutting you off?"

"Yeah."

"Who we pose' to get our work from then?"

"Imma holla at my man Fy Heed from Delaware."

"That's some Fucked up shit Zoey on, after all tha money we made for her."

"Her lost not ours, I think it's time to take this shit over."

"You sure you wanna do this, she is ya family?"

"Fuck her! All that family shit is out of tha window and if she don't like it, too bad! Matter fact, I will give her a heads up."

"What?"

"I said what I had to say."

"Nah I just wanted you to know you started this shit and not me."

CLICK!

"Zoey, what did he say now?"

"That I started this…not him."

"I had a feeling it was going to come to this."

"I need to call everybody to set up a meeting."

"I don't think that will be a good ideal."

"And why not?"

"Do you want everybody to know what's going down?"

"Zell, I could care less what everybody knows."

"Would if they try you?"

"Listen Zell, they respect and fear me, but if I don't tell them then they will continue to buy shit fromJibbs thinking it's mine."

"Oh shit! I didn't think about that."

After I called up everybody, we went to go meet wit them.

"I called you all here to let you know that Jibbs is now doing his own thing."

"So that's why he called me and said that tha price might be going up."

"He called me too." Come to find out he called almost everybody.

"So are yall beefing?"

"I'm not going to lie, he was dealing wit some people that I told him not to deal wit and lied to me about it, so I cut him off."

"Zoey I know that's ya peoples, but you better watch him.

"Yeah cause on some real shit, I was only dealing wit him on tha strength of you."

"From here on out you'll deal wit me, Tweek, or Cal."

Cal and Tweek both looked at me surprised, I just smiled at them both. Before we left we made sure everybody had our numbers. *I thought to myself, I need to call Javier so we can switch to another storage spot.*

Cal and Tweek met us at Ms. Tootsies for lunch tha next day.

"So do you think Jibbs will be on some dumb shit?"

"For his sake I hope not," Tweek answered before Zoey could respond.

"I know thats ya family, but I'm not going to sit back and let him do nothin to you or Zell."

"You of all people should know that I could take care of myself."

"Cal do you think you can handle this new position?"

"Can a dog bark?"

"What you laughing at Tweek?

"Dat nigga funny as shit, talkin bout do dogs bark."

"On some real shit, Zoey I can handle it, but I do have a block to run."

"I'm sure between tha two of you it shouldn't be a problem."

"I haven't seen ya boy Box around lately.

Zoey you know I don't Fuck wit dat nigga no more."

"What does that have to do wit me seeing him around? I got a shipment coming in tomorrow, so make sure ya schedule is clear between 10 and 1."

"You got it Boss."

"Tweek, don't play wit me, I'm not ya boss."

"Why you always takin everything to heart."

I just gave him that look that said I'll deal wit you later.

"Stop, don't try and kiss me now."

"Awe, is my Baby mad?"

"Zoey I'm thinking about throwing Ciara surprise birthday party."

"What is there to think about, lets do it."

"Yeah, I'm always down for a good party, especially my cousins," Zell said dapping Cal.

"I can get Riz to call up that chick that made those fliers for Quez that time."

"Do that."

"I need a picture of her for tha flyer."

"I'll get it to you today or tomorrow."

"Make sure its a recent picture and not from 95."

"Ha! Ha! Ha! Oh you got jokes huh?"

"No, but I know Ciara hasn't took a picture in years."

"Not since Calry was 2, but it's a pretty one so I'll use that."

"I'm bout to route, I have a few things to take care of Tweek, I'll see you on tha block.

"A'ight. Zoey I'll see you tomorrow."

"Zoey I'll call you later, I gotta take Mom Rosslynn to tha salon.

"OK call me later."

"Well I guess it's just me and you smart ass."

"Damn you still holding on?"

"You already know how I am."

"I'm sorry Baby, give me a kiss."

"Nope."

"Well, let me pay for lunch then."

"Now that you can do. No, but seriously I don't want you to think of me as ya boss because I'm not."

"I know, you are Wifey. There goes that smile I love."

Everybody turned to look at tha commotion at tha front of tha store. In tha words of Wendy Williams 'HOW YOU DOIN'," Zoey said in reference to tha Spanish and White homosexuals causing a scene.

"Lets go, I've scene more than enough."

"I need you to give me a ride to my car I rode wit Cal."

"Where is ya car at?"

"In front of my house. Are you up for a movie later or do you have plans?"

"I don't have any plans, just hit me and let me know what time tha movie starts.

"Will do."

After I dropped Tweek off I went to pay my electric and cable bill.

"Look at this mafucka he ain't shit." Jibbs and LT was standing on tha corner talking like they were tha best of friends. I decided to park down tha block and give Jibbs a call.

"What?"

"Damn that's how you feel?"

"Zoey what do you want? I don't have time for this I'm busy."

"Jibbs I just want to know if you're really dealing wit LT and Roscoe?"

"I told you before that I wasn't."

"So you have never talked to either of them outside of that day at tha restaurant?"

"Nope." I pulled out from my parking spot and when I got to where they were standing, I yelled "LIAR" and hung up.

"Damn what this bitch following me now?"

"Who is that?"

"Zoey."

"Oh shit! I didn't even recognize her."

"She been on some bullshit tha past few days because she found out I was dealin wit you and Roscoe."

"I hollered at my folks in Delaware so everything is still everything."

"So you should be ready to make that move then?"

"Yup, in about another week or two."

"That's all it is then."

"Do you think them niggaz is gonna ride wit her?"

"I doubt it, I already let 'em know that numbers might go up a little and they were cool wit it, besides they don't know I'm not down wit her anymore." So he thought.

"Well you already know that I'm down wit you, so just give ya boy tha word and she's history."

"Slow ya roll Baby Boy, I'm not going to kill her, just crush her and anything or one who gets in my way, along tha way."

"I just want to be prepared because if she finds out its on."

"I'm well aware of that; I have to go meet wit my people, so I'll hit you up once everything is everything."

"My phone will be on, be safe."

"Always."

"Jibbs my man, long time no see or hear from."

"I know, I've been handlin biz-ness. So what can I do for you?"

"What ya numbers looking like now?"

"It depends on what you're try'n to cop a brick or more."

"28 grand a piece, but if you grab 5 or better I'll let them go at 26 a piece."

"That's only a stack more than I was playing wit Zoey," thought to

myself.

"Let me get 10 of them."

"Damn you really stepped ya game up from tha ½ bird you was copping."

"I had to step my game up, I love money."

When you are ready just hit my phone."

"I'm ready when ever you are."

"A'ight, give me about an hour."

"A'ight, Imma just hang out down here."

"Where's a good spot to eat at?"

"Do you know where 5th and Madison is?"

"Yeah…yeah I think. Is that by that center?"

"Yeah, I got a steak shop over there, trust me is tha best. I'll call my peeps and let them know you're on ya way, it's on me."

"Any particular meal I should order?"

"No. everything on tha menu is blazing."

"Well hit me when you're ready."

"Just leave ya car unlocked and I'll put it under tha driver seat."

"That's what's up."

I pulled up in front of tha steak shop just as someone was pulling out. I looked at tha menu, there were a lot of different foods to choose from and after five minutes, I decided on tha cheese steak and shrimp platter.

"Your name is," tha old man wit tha red beard asked me?

"He said that ya money is no good here and he would see you in a little while. You can have my seat, I'll call you when ya order is up."

"I'm going next door to grab a Dutch."

"Take ya time."

I brought a Dutch and then rolled up a blunt of Kush I had in tha car. I went back in tha shop at tha and finished smoking my Dutch.

"I was just about to come and get you," Mr. Red said coming from behind tha counter wit my food.

"Wow this is really good." Fy Heed walked in wit some dude.

"I see you enjoying ya meal."

"Fy Heed I can't front, you definitely got something on ya hands wit this joint."

"I know, I have people from all over, come to eat here."

"Word."

"Word. I was even in tha top 5 places to eat on Oprah."

"If you was on Oprah, that's major!"

"Some important people told some important people and the next thing I know my wife called me saying my shop was on Oprah.No wonder people are coming from all over to eat here, you know once Oprah puts her stamp on something, it's an instant hit."

"Well let me get back up tha highway."

"Be easy."

"Always, I'll hit you up when I finish."

"Cool." I put tha work in my stash spot and hit tha highway.

"Yo."

"What's up Bo?"

"Just making sure you OK, you've been down there for a minute."

"I'm on 95 now, be there in 15."

"I'll be at tha spot when you get there.

When I walked in Bo had everything already ready. I got straight to biz-ness and everything came back.

"Let me hit these niggaz up to let them know it's on."

By tha time I finished calling, everybody was pissed because they all had just grabbed from Zoey, but I still let them know I had them for 30 grand which was only 2 stacks more than they were paying now.

"Jibbs do you really think they gonna go for that?"

"What choice do they have?"

"Bo they don't even have Zoey's number, so they can't call her to confirm it."

"Yeah I guess you're right."

"I'm always right nigga."

"Did you find out who hit those spots yet?"

"Nah, but I got some of my broads on top of it."

"Keep me posted on that."

"I need to make a few drops, so I'll hit you up later."

"A'ight Imma be on tha block dumping this work." My first step was at tha bar on 6th and Berks to drop off some work to Mr. Vince.

"I was just about to call you, my peoples we're starting to get a little impatient."

"Since when do we let our customers control tha tempo?"

"Here tha numbers is up 2 stacks."

"As long as its good, I don't care."

"Come on now, its me you talkin to."

"Say no more."

"Hit me when you done."

"Don't I always?"

"True dat, true dat."

As I was walking out tha bar I saw some dude walking up to another dude wit a pistol in his hand.

"Yo nigga didn't I tell you to take that shit somewhere else?"

"Man I ain't doing noth...BOOM!" Before he could finish half his face was on tha ground.

BOOM! BOOM! BOOM!

Just to make sure he was dead, dude hit him 3 more times, two in tha chest and one more in tha head. I just walked to my car, got in and pulled off as if I didn't just see a nigga get his shit pushed back.

CHAPTER 36

Jibbs Try'n to Sell tha Work for More

"Yo, Jibbs called me."

"What he want?"

"Said that he was ready.

"He doesn't think we know about him and Zoey?"

"I should tell him to bring me 10 then rob his Bitch ass for try'n to play me."

"That ain't gonna do nothin but start some shit."

"Fuck that nigga!"

"I'm wit you on that, but we don't need no beef right now."

"Won't be no beef if I just push his shit back."

"You gotta pump ya brakes."

"Nigga that bitch got you getting soft."

"Don't nobody got me getting soft, I'm just wiser now. Remember tha other day when I had to send that Jamaican nigga to tha bone yard?"

"Yeah what about it?"

"Jibbs was coming out tha bar."

"Did he see you?"

"If he did, we wouldn't be having a conversation about him."

"Did you hit Cal up and let him know what Jibbs is try'n to do?"

"Yeah, he said he would let Zoey know about it. And on tha strength of you, I'll let that nigga live."

"Don't say on tha strength of me cause I dont give a Fuck if he live or die!"

"No more said."

"Hello."

"What up Sis?"

"Hey, I got those fliers for you."

"Oh that's what's up, but Lucky just called me."

"What he say?"

"Jibbs is try'n to sell them work for 2 stacks more.

"They already know what tha deal is, so he won't be selling that shit and just to be smart hit everybody and let them know tha price just dropped to 26 grand."

"They're gonna love that."

"If Jibbs wants to play dirty, I'll make it hard for him to eat."

"Imma send tha fliers wit Tweek."

"A'ight I'll talk to you later."

"What was that about?"

"None of ya biz-ness."

"My sister is my biz-ness."

"Well, if she wants you to know, she'll tell you."

"I guess I'll have to just call her then."

"Be my guest," I said handing her tha house phone.

"What Ciara? And no I'm not telling you what we were talking about."

"Damn, how you know what I want?"

"Because I just got off tha phone wit Cal."

"So now yall keeping secrets?"

"No."

"I can't tell."

"If you must really know, I needed to know something about Tweek."

"I had a feeling that's what it was about because he would have told me."

"He doesn't tell you everything."

"Yes he does." *If he did you would know I was in tha game, I thought to myself.*

"So what are you doing for your big day?""

"I don't know, probably going to dinner then to some club."

"You club? Yeah right."

"I can still party wit tha best of 'em."

"I didn't say you couldn't, you just haven't been since Calry was born."

"I know right. Well let me get off this phone I have to get to tha shop."

"A'ight stop by later.

"Oh yeah before I forget, me and Cal are going away at tha end of next month to Punta Canta. Do you and Tweek want to go?"

"I have to ask Tweek, but even if he doesn't, count me in."

"OK, but get back wit me before tha end of next week so I can make tha reservations."

"I'll let you know later when I stop by."

When I walked into tha shop Tweek was getting his hair braided.

"Hey sexy," he said over tha talking and music.

"When you get done come in my office, I need to talk to you."

"Zoey I put those invoices on your desk."

"Thanks Acis."

"No problem, you just missed Aunt Zelda."

"She told me she had an appointment wit you today."

"I told her she didn't have to make an appointment, just come in."

"You know she's not going to do that."

"I know, she said she didn't want any special treatment just because she's my aunt."

I hadn't been to tha shop in a week so I had some work to catch up on. KNOCK! KNOCK!

"Come in."

"Hey you want to go to Punta Canta wit me, my sister and Cal next month?"

"Cal asked me tha same thing last week."

"Did he?"

"Yeah, I told him I was going to ask you but it slipped my mind."

"So I'll take that as a yes then."

"Of course, like I'm going to pass up on tha chance to see you in a bikini."

"Oh so that's tha only reason you going?"

"No that's not tha only reason, but it's one of them."

"Boy you gon' make me hurt you."

"In that case let me get outta here, I'll see you later," he said blowing me a kiss. I grabbed it outta tha air and put it on my lips.

I've been wit Tweek for almost a year and he has not once tried to have sex wit me, which makes me respect him more. I already had my mind made up that he would be getting some of this good pussy in tha Dominican Republic.

CHAPTER 37

Ciara is Going to be Surprised

"Unh, unh, unh."

"What?"

"You look beautiful."

"Thank you, you're lookin quite handsome ya self." And he was wit his brown Gucci blazer wit matching loafers and Gucci jeans wit a white button up.

"Biggie said it best, 'Stay Gucci down to tha socks.'"

"Boy you crazy."

"Ciara is going to be surprised when she walks in tonight."

"I know, she thinks they're just going to a club."

"Let me finish getting dressed".

"Don't be all night Slow Poke."

"Whaaaaat ever."

Ten minutes later Zoey came down tha steps looking like something fresh off tha Americas Top Model runway wit a pink and cream Zac Posen dress and matching pink stilettos.

"Close ya mouth before something flies in it."

"Wow you look beautiful, I'm gonna have to fight tha niggaz off tonight."

"No you won't, I'm all yours."

"I know that and you know that, but them wolves don't."

"Trust me, after tonight they will."

"Oh yeah? How is that?"

"Cause Imma be on ya arm like a tattoo."

"Sounds good."

"You'll see."

"Baby are you ready?"

"Just about, I'm putting on my shoes, OK I'm ready now."

"I forgot to give you this…Happy Birthday Baby." I opened up tha box and was at a lost for words.

"Ooooooh my God!"

"I guess that means you like it?"

"Like it? Daddy I love it!" I could tell that he spent some money on this diamond necklace wit my name in all diamonds.

"Let me put that on for you."

My necklace completed my outfit; I had on a cream Max Azria dress wit a pair of brown Givenchy pumps.

"Ciara we better get outta here before we don't make it nowhere tonight."

"Shiiiit…as good as I look, I'm showing this outfit off tonight."

"Did my sister say she was coming out tonight?"

"Yeah, her, Tweek, Zell and Spence is s'pose to meet us there."

"Did you roll up some of that weed you be smokin?"

"Why?"

"Cause I want to smoke some." He passed me tha blunt as we were going out tha door.

"I am what you call an occasion smoker…always smoke on occasion and this being one.

"Don't hurt ya self wit that."

"Boy please…just cause I don't smoke every day don't mean I can't handle it."

"I'm just saying, that is top of tha line." I could tell it was top of tha line because I was high as shit after just 3 pulls.

"Damn it must be jumpin in there tonight, look at tha line."

"Don't worry, we not waiting in line." We parked in tha lot down tha street from tha club.

"Zoey and Zell are already inside, there goes their cars." I pulled my phone out to call and let them know we were on our way in.

"Excuse us, excuse us," Cal said as we walked to tha front of tha line.

"Go ahead in Cal, Happy Birthday Ciara." I looked at Cal, who just looked at me and shrugged his shoulders.

We walked in only to be met by Tweek, Zell, Zoey, Spence, Aunt Masiah. and my mom.

"What are you doing here?"

"We aren't allowed to celebrate ya birthday wit you?"

"Of course, but Cal didn't say you were coming out."

"Tha birthday girl has entered tha building, Happy Birthday Ciara."

"Huh?"

"You heard him…this is ya party," Tweek said giving her a flyer.

"You mean to tell me yall planned this?"

"Sure did," Zell said wit a big smile.

"Mom you and Aunt Siah knew and didn't tell me?"

"Now what kinda surprised would it have been if you knew about it?"Jibbs and Bo walked up. "Happy Birthday Cuz," he said handing her some money.

"Thank you Jibbs," she said hugging him in return.

Cal, Tweek, Zoey, Zell…we all just said what's up, nothing more.

After they walked away Ciara asked,"What was up wit that?"

"What's that Sis?"

"Nevermind, we'll talk tomorrow…let's party."

"I told you I would be on your arm all night."

"If you want to do ya thing, go ahead."

"You must be try'n to get rid of me.'

"No not at all, but I don't wanna stop you from having a good time."

"I'm fine trust me."

"Well say no more…let's get a drink."

GIRL YOU GOING THINK, GIRL YOU GOING THINK, GIRL YOU GOING TO THINK…

"Awwwww shit! That's my song come on Cal."

"Mom look at ya daughter."

"Chile, I see her, she's enjoying herself for a change."

GO SHORTY IT'S YA BIRTHDAY AND WE GON PARTY LIKE IT'S YA BIRTHDAY AND WE DON'T GIVE A FUCK CAUSE IT'S YA BIRTHDAY…"Hey yall heard what 50 said it's my birthday, Heeeey!" I enjoyed seeing my sister having fun, its been awhile since she's been anywhere besides work, moms or tha grocery store. Just when everything was going good, 2 females started fighting over some dude. Tha bouncers quickly broke it up and escorted them out of tha club. We took some pictures so we could remember this night. By tha end of tha night Ciara was pissy drunk.

"Oh my God I'm drunk as shit."

"You think," I said laughing my ass off.

"Thank yall…I really, really enjoyed myself tonight. Where's Aunt Siah and mommy at?"

"They left an hour ago."

"So they couldn't hang?" When tha party was over, we all made our way to tha exit where tha rest of tha people were exiting.

"Listen, I'm not try'n to hear that Bitch, either you have my money by tomorrow or."

"Or what nigga? I don't owe you shit!"

"You must think this is a game."

"Zoey is that Jibbs?"

"Yeah."

"Come on let's get him before he gets into trouble." I grabbed her by tha arm, he's grown and that don't have shit to do wit us.

"You gave that shit to my brother not me."

"Yeah, but you cosigned for him."

"I did but he's locked up."

"For child support not my shit…so I need my money."

"You need to take that up wit him."

"Don't have my money tomorrow, that's all Imma say!"

I pulled out my phone to make a quick call.

"Yo whats up man?"

"How much does ya brother owe him?"

"I don't know and really don't care."

"I know but there's no need for no bullshit."

"I feel you but you got me Fucked up."

"Just ask him what he owes him."

"Hold up, what he owe you?"

"6500."

"Tell him you'll hit him tomorrow at noon."

"Nah, I'll pay tha tab…don't worry about it."

"Who was that?"

"I called to make sure mommy and Aunt Siah made it home safely."

"Listen Jibbs, I'll hit you at 12 tomorrow."

"I know you will."

I was about to pull out my pistol when tha police pulled up and told everybody to clear out. Jibbs doesn't know how close he was to checking out.

"Ciara!Ciara!"

"Oh my God! Will you please stop yelling, my head hurts."

"Ha! Ha! Ha!"

"What's so funny?"

"I told you not to mix that Remy wit that Bombay."

"I know and I should have listened because now I'm paying tha price wit this hangover."

"Here drink this."

"Wheeeew…is this liquor?"

"Yeah."

"I'm not trying to get drunk all over again."

"Just drink it, it's an old hangover remedy." She took tha glass and gulped it down.

"Wheeeew…that shit is strong."

"Now go get in tha shower and you'll will be back to normal."

"Oh yeah, ya mom and Zoey said to call when you get ya self together."

"OK."

"I'm bout to pick Calry up and take him out for awhile."

"Thank you."

"For what?"

"Last night, I had a ball, you might of started something.

"Well you need to get out more and have fun."

"Now you sound like Zell and Zoey."

"Baby all you do is work, work, work."

"No I don't…I make sure you in Calry have a home cooked meal every night and that you come home to a clean house." When I started to smile all she could say was point taken.

"Hello."

"Hey did you take care of that for me?"

"Yeah, I just dropped it off."

"Thanks."

"No problem, but I still don't see why you paid Jibbs that money."

"Simple…if I didn't somebody would be dead."

"Zoey, I don't know if it's even my place to say anything, but Jibbs is starting to make a lot of enemies, me included."

"Cal where are you at now?"

"Just pulled up to tha block."

"Meet me at tha Food Court in tha Gallery."

"Be there in 15, 20 minutes tops."

20 minutes later I was walking into tha Gallery and headed down tha escalator to tha Food Court. I spotted Zoey at a table by tha Chinese Restaurant.

"Hey, I didn't want to talk on tha phone and since I was already here..."

"It ain't no problem."

"Now what's going on wit you and Jibbs, I thought yall were cool?"

"So did I, but a few of my peoples said that he was throwing dirt on me."

"What kinda dirt?"

"He called some people to let them know he was holding and when they said they were dealing wit me, he went on about how if it wasn't for him and I got his shit anyway."

"Zoey, I never had a problem wit Jibbs and I didn't ask to be put in this position."

"No you didn't, but now that you are, you have to be able to take what comes wit it."

"I can take what ever, but I won't take any disrespect from anybody, not even Jibbs!" Zoey's phone started to ring.

"Hold up for a second…hello."

"Hey Sis you busy?"

"A little why? Is everything a'ight?"

"Yeah, Cal just told me you said to call when I got myself together."

"I did."

"Well finish what ever you were doing and hit me later."

"I'll stop by when I leave tha mall."

"You should have called, I would've went wit you."

"Un hello…I did call, but you were hungover. Ha! Ha! Ha!"

"Very funny, Ha! Ha! Ha!"

"You sure don't sound hungover."

"My Baby gave me something that took it away."

"Eeeeell."

"Not that, maybe if you got some you would not always be thinking about it."

Bye…I'll see you in a little while."

"That was ya soon to be Wifey? Cal Imma holla at Jibbs and see what's up wit him."

"Zoey tha word on tha street is that Jibbs is try'n to be tha man and wit out him you wouldn't be where you are.

"He didn't do shit, Quez started this. I just took tha torch and kept it burning; so wit or wit out him I would've been straight."

"Tha only reason he didn't want me involved was cause if he tried to take over, nobody would question it."

"That worked out well for him."

"All I'm saying is…keep ya eyes and ears open. I no longer trust him or Box."

"Well, I better get to moms and that new shipment came in today."

"Oh OK…I was just about to ask you about that.

For tha next few days Jibbs was running down on everybody try'n to get them to cop from him.

"I see now, Zoey is going to be a problem."

"There is only one way to deal wit a problem."

"I didn't go through all this bullshit to have her thinking she's that Bitch."

"Well it's time we show her and everybody else who's really runnin this city."

"I heard from my sister that her, Cal, Tweek and Ciara are going away in two weeks and you know what they say."

"What's that?"

"While tha cats away tha mice will play and we gon' play hard."

CHAPTER 38

Stick ups Instead of Hustling

1, 2, 3 BOOM! "EVERYBODY DOWN NOW FBI! GET DOWN AND DON'T MOVE! Somebody go secure tha rest of tha house!"

"I want to see a Search Warrant."

"You'll see it when you see tha Judge…now Shut tha Fuck up! Matter of fact, I'll even leave a copy on tha table for you to look at."

"All secure KC!" yelled from upstairs.

We then proceeded to search tha entire crib until we found what we came to get. I looked inside tha 2 duffle bags satisfied, then I walked downstairs.

"We appreciate tha donations, yall have a nice day!"

"I knew those mafuckas wasn't Feds!" one of tha guys yelled out.

We hit two more small spots then made our way back to tha Stash House to divide tha profits.

"Just imagine if we were doing this all those years instead of hustling, we would really be paid."

"I'm paid now, over tha past 6½ months I went from nothing to now being worth close to a million dollars, talk about coming up." We all came out wit $75,000, 4 bricks and 10 pounds of weed a piece to add to our growing stashes.

"I've been hitting Balinda's cousin Shane wit all tha work I been getting from tha stick ups."

"KC you gon' buy these jawns too?"

"Yeah, let me get all 8 of 'em, but I'm gonna owe one of yall 5 stacks.”

“Nah, we even on tha 5, I owe you.”

“Shit! I forgot all about that.”

“Damn, I shouldn’t have said nothing about that.”

“Too late now nigga,” I said throwing a jab at him.

“I meant to ask yall if yall wanted to hit Cal and Tweek for some real money this time?”

“I’m down, tha way they eating all crazy now.”

“Word is they hooked up wit some Colombian cat who’s hitting them wit major weight and I do mean major.”

“Well let’s do our homework and do what we do. I gotta drop this work off then pick Balinda up from work.”

“Her car is in tha shop again?”

“Yeah.”

“If you don’t just buy her a new car.”

“She won’t let me.”

“Then surprise her wit one, it’s not like she gon’ tell you to take it back.”

“Box I knew you was good for something besides robbing niggaz.”

“Fuck you KC! Here’s a thought, I was going to tha auction tomorrow why don’t you join me.”

“I will, I know I can find something real nice and reliable.”

“Meet me here after you drop Balinda off at work.”

“A’ight.”

“I’ll get up wit yall, I got a hot date in a few hours.”

“Don’t tell me you ain’t knock Shorty off yet.”

"Awe this nigga try'n to wife her Box."

"Damn right! I am, not only is she bad as a mafucka, and she's not out there, so why not snatch her up. Respect, respect. Plus you and Box got wifey's so I figured I'd join tha club. Ha! Ha! Ha! Let me get up outta here before I'm late then I'll never hear tha end of it."

"I'm outta here too, I have to pick Shay up for dinner."

"I was just about to call you."

"I don't know why, I'm not late."

"I know I was going to tell you to stop and get me some McDonalds on ya way, I'm starving."

"Let's go to tha Bottom of tha Sea."

"I could go for some steam shrimp."

"Say no more, anything for my Baby."

"Now you got me blushing." Two hours later we were both stuffed like a turkey.

"Damn I am so full, all I wanna do is take a hot bath and lay down."

"Do you have to do anything tonight?"

"I just gotta drop some shit off to Shane, why?"

"I wanted you to stay wit me tonight."

"No problem, when is ya car going to be finished?"

"Why…you tired of dropping me off and picking me up?"

"No, but it might be a time when I can't pick you up, like tomorrow."

"I'll catch tha bus."

"No you won't hold on..." I pulled out my phone and called Glass, when he didn't answer I called Box.

"Yo."

"Can you pick me up from Balinda's in tha morning?"

"Don't tell me ya car is on tha fritz too."

"Nah, Imma let her take my car just in case we not done when she gets off."

"A'ight, I'll be by at 9 so be ready."

"You got it Playboy."

"Baby you can take my car, Box is going to pick me up in tha morning."

"I would've caught tha bus, you don't have to inconvenience yourself for me."

"Stop talking stupid, what I look like letting you catch tha bus."

I'm just saying you..."

"You not saying nothing, you taking my car, end of discussion," I said not letting her finish her sentence.

"Well that's all it is then." We ended up watching a movie then going to bed.

Tha next morning Balinda woke me up before she left for work. No soon as I got myself together Box was out front blowing tha horn like a mad man.

"OK! OK! Lay off tha horn nigga."

"My fault, I thought you would still be sleep." We stopped at McDonalds to grab something to eat before heading to meet Glass.

"You niggaz didn't have to grab me nothing."

"We know, that's why we didn't."

"Come on so we can get first dibbs on tha cars we like."

"I guess everybody was thinking tha same thing," Box said referring to all tha people that were already there.

"Yeah, I guess so."

By 11 o'clock I purchased two cars a 94' Caprice Classic for me and a Dodge Charger fully loaded wit a set of Dueces for Balinda.

"I'm ready to roll before I end up buying something else."

"Me too," Box said he copped a Silver Buick Lucerne while Glass grabbed a Infinity G37.

"Nigga let me find out Shawty got you hooked like a fish and you ain't even smash yet."

"Fuck you nigga!"

"I'm just say'n you brought that car for her, didn't you?"

"Why you try'n to carry me?"

"Nigga he just asked you a question."

"Yall know I did, I told yall I was."

"Mafucka you ain't tell us shit."

"Awe nigga you buying Balinda a whip too?"

"I know and she's wifey."

"So is Talia."

"Well that explains it, I didn't know you actually wifed her, I thought you were still try'n."

"How much did you say you get paid for thinking again?"

"Ha! Ha! Ha! Very funny mafucka."

"I thought it was."

"Nigga you think every thing funny."

"He didn't think it was funny when Shawty hit his car."

"Ha! Ha! Ha! Now that was some funny ass shit."

"Yup, I'll be laughing all tha way to tha bank when my lawsuit comes." We took care of all tha paperwork then left.

We got Box to drive us back so we could get our other cars. I parked Balinda's car in tha driveway then put a big red bow on it.

"Oh my God! Oh my God! I know KC did not buy me a new car!"

I walked into tha house expecting to see KC sitting on tha couch wit that gorgeous smile on his face that I love so much, but instead I was greeted by a note tape to tha TV.

Dear Balinda,

I'm sorry I couldnt be here to see tha look on ya face when you walked through tha door, but I'm sure it was all smiles. Tha keys to ya car are on tha counter. Oh yeah, there's something in tha trunk for you. I'll be by to pick you up at 8 o'clock so please be ready.

Love KC

I couldn't get tha keys to my new car fast enough. When I got to tha trunk I opened it only to be greeted by a box wit a bow on it. I waited until I got back in tha house to open it.

"Oh my God, this is tha Christian Dior dress I wanted to go wit my shoes I brought last weekend."

He even had a single rose inside tha box. I couldn't wait to put that dress on and feel tha fabric on my skin. Two and a half hours later I was dressed and waiting on my Knight in Shining Armor or in this case in Gucci.

HONK! HONK! HONK!

"I'm coming! Ease off tha horn!"

"I see I'm not tha only one wit a new car."

"I had to have this, I been looking for one of these for a while now."

"Did it come wit these rims?"

"Nah I put these 24's on today, but ya car came wit those Dueces."

"Baby thank you," she said leaning over to kiss me, "what am I going to do wit my old car?"

"Sell it."

"I'm not selling my car."

"Well give it to ya little sistah."

"Now I can do that because she's been bugging me for my car anyway."

"How much does it cost to have it fixed?"

"I aready paid for it."

"Then sell it to ya sis for a hundred bucks."

"A hundred bucks!"

"Yeah."

"No Imma sell it to her for 1,500, what I paid to have it fixed, she's got it."

"How you know she got it?"

"Cause she just told me she was try'n to buy a car for two stacks or less."

We pulled up to tha pier where we were having dinner. By tha end of tha night we both were a little tipsy.

"Baby I really enjoyed dinner tonight thank you."

"You deserve tha best, I let you go once and I'm not going to do it again."

"KC you don't have to shower me wit gifts to keep me, I'm wit you because I love you and I never stopped."

(Talia gets her new car from Glass)

"Oh my God! This is really my car?"

"Unless you don't want it, it's yours."

"Of course I want it, now I don't have to keep calling you or my mom to take or pick me up from work. Glass what did I do to deserve you?"

"Talia all you did was be you."

"Who else was I suppose to be?"

"I'm use to dealing wit money hungry broads and for tha seven months we have been together, you never asked me for anything."

"Except a ride to and from work."

"You won't be doing that any more."

"Glass I don't want to run you off, but I need to tell you something."

"I knew she was to good to be true," I thought to myself.

"You don't have to look like that, I just wanted to let you know that I love you." I was at a loss for words.

"I understand if you don't feel tha same way."

"Actually, I love you too Talia."

Next thing I knew we were making love for tha first time and if I didn't know before I definitely knew now I was in love wit her.

Ever since I met Shay at Toys R' Us we've been messing. We were good together, she didn't press me for any money and I didn't press her for sex. Tonight we were going to tha Laugh House to check out Mike Epps.

"Ha! Ha! Ha!"

He had both of us laughing our asses off. At tha end of tha show Shay got tha chance to meet him and get his autograph.

"I really needed that, my job stressed me out today."

"I told you not to let those people do that to you."

"I know, but they do."

"When I open my biz-ness you can work for me."

"Work for you huh?"

"Yeah, what would be wrong wit that?"

"I would rather be part owner."

"Oh you got part owner money."

"I'm sitting on a little something, something."

"Word?"

"I ain't no broke Bitch!"

"I never said you were."

"I'm just making sure you know it Boop-Boop"

"What I tell you bout calling me that?"

"Pleeeease you are my Boop-Boop."

"Just don't call me that in public or in front of my Boys."

"You think it might tarnish ya thug appeal?"

"I'm not worried about that, I just don't want Glass and KC running around calling me that."

"Boy you on image time, I don't say nothing about you calling me

Babygirl."

"If it will make you happy call me what you want."

"It's not like I haven't been calling you that for tha past 5½ months.

"Yeah and I've been say'n tha same shit for 5½ months."

"Are you staying wit me tonight or do you have things to do?"

"Only if you want me to."

"Boy stop playing wit me." I stopped at tha store to get some Purple Haze Wraps since I wouldn't be going back out tonight.

CHAPTER 39

The Vacation in tha Dominican

"Wow, it's beautiful here."

"I know, look how blue tha water is."

I tapped Tweek when this bad ass Dominican chick walked by wit a fat ass. All he could do was smile.

"Don't get Fucked up Tweek!"

"What did I do now?"

"I saw tha way you was staring at that broad."

"You mean tha same way you're staring at him," I said pointing to tha Dominican dude that was standing across from us.

"Look we came to enjoy ourselves and there are going to be a lot of beautiful woman and handsome men here."

"He's right and there it's nothing wrong wit looking as long as we don't touch."

Ciara looked at Zoey and then said, "Remember you said that."

"Zoey all I have to say is. don't be disrespectful looking."

"Tell ya self that," she said punching me in my arm.

"Ouch!"

"Boy that did not hurt, so stop playing."

"Did I ever tell you how gorgeous you are when you get upset?"

"Only a thousand times."

"Well that was a thousand and one."

"Yall are so crazy, we better check in.

"I don't know about you, but I wanna find some weed."

"Unh, unh, unh, all yall wanna do is smoke."

While we were checking in I noticed tha Bell Hop was high.

"My man you speak English?"

"Yeah what's up, Papi?"

"Where can I get some good smoke from?"

"How much you try'n to get?"

"Depends on tha price."

"Take ya stuff to your room then come back down and holla at me."

"You determined ain't you?"

"Damn right, I need to smoke." Once we were settled in I went back down to see Papi.

"Papi I'm here for two weeks, so I need at least a quarter pound of tha best shit."

"Tha best shit is going to cost you a pretty penny."

"As long as it's tha best tha price ain't no problem."

"I get off in 15 minutes."

"A'ight I'm in room 616."

"I'll get it and bring it up."

"How much?"

"500."

"It must be really good for that price."

"Tha best Papi tha best." 45 minutes later we were all sitting around smoking.

"Damn this some good shit. Papi wasn't bullshit'n."

We had a ball that night. Tha next morning we got up and had breakfast, then got ready to go scuba diving.

"Oh my God, did you see how big that fish was?"

"How could I not, it swam right next to me."

"I thought Zoey was gonna have a heart attack in tha water."

"Baby ya eyes got big like golf balls. Ha! Ha! Ha!"

"So that was funny huh?"

"Yeah and I got tha picture to prove it."

"No you didn't."

"Yes I did."

"I don't know bout yall, but I wanna smoke."

"Listen to you, every since ya birthday you been smoking a lot. Let me find out my big Sis is a weed head."

"I'm not a weed head, I just like good weed."

"Let me ask you a few questions."

"I'm listening."

"Do you smoke everyday?"

"No."

"Uhah, Uhuh," Cal said clearing his throat.

"OK I do, but only one Dutch."

"If it's not high grade do you snap?"

"Of course, I'm not smoking no dirt."

"Do you buy tha weed?"

"No Cal does."

"Yeah, but you give me tha money," said Cal.

"Do you have ya own stash?"

"Damn...what are you wired?"

"Just answer tha question, do you have ya own stash?"

"Yes."

"Yup, she's definitely a weed head."

"Tsss...what ever," I said sucking my teeth.

"C ain't nothing wrong wit being a weed head."

"I know Sis, we have something in common now," Zoey said lighting up a big ass Dutch.

That night we went to this night club tha Bell Hop told us about, to our surprise they played a lot of hip hop.

"I don't know about yall, but I'm ready to go back to tha hotel."

"Tweek let me find out you can't hang."

"C I'm tore up, I need to be rested for tomorrow. Yall can stay if yall want to."

"Nah lets go."

As soon as we got back to our room I jumped in tha shower.

"You don't mind if I join you do you?" I looked up to see Zoey standing there wit a towel around her.

"Why would I mind?"

Wit that said she dropped tha towel and got in. Me and Zoey have been together for a year and this is my first time seeing her naked.

"Why are you looking at me like that?"

"Because ya body is flawless."

"Now you got me blushing." I didn't even try anything I just washed her and then got out. *I see I'm going to have to take control," I thought to myself as I was drying off.*

"Baby can you lotion my back for me please?" After he was done he laid back on tha bed wit a Dutch his mouth. I knew Tweek would not try to have sex with me that's why I respected him so much.

"Baby let me give you a nice rub down."

"So now you a mind reader huh?"

"If you was thinkin' that, why didn't you just ask?" He just smiled and started to turn over.

"Unh, Unh stay on ya back." I started rubbing his shoulders.

"Damn why you so tense? We on vacation you should be relaxed."

"I am relaxed."

As I continued to you to massage him I noticed his FRIEND was starting to grow so I took tha opportunity to stroke him. Ummm was tha sound that escaped his mouth. I decided that I might as well give him tha royal treatment. As soon as I slid my tongue on tha tip of his shaft his eyes rolled in tha back of his head. When he pushed my head I thought that maybe he wasn't enjoying it. Before I could ask what was wrong I was on my back.

"Ssssh! Just lay back, let me take care of you and your needs." All I could do was smile to myself as he began to rub my body. When I felt his tongue on my neck it caused me to jump a little.

"Are you a'ight?"

Yes." I continued to run my tongue along her neck moving down to her chest. Once there I ran tha tip of my tongue across her nipple causing her to let out a soft moan. Not wanting to stop I continued down her body licking her inner thigh until I reached the spot I needed to be. As soon as I licked her clit she let out a loud moan.

"Oh my God!" I couldn't believe how good he had me feeling, after about 10 minutes I felt my body trembling.

"Ummm Baby I'm Cumming!" That made him lick and suck even harder causing me to have multiple orgasms.

"Hold on! Hold on," I said getting up to get tha condoms I had brought along out of my bag.

She threw me tha condoms, but I wasn't ready to put them on yet. I told her to lay on her stomach so that I could eat it from tha back. I had to laugh to myself because Zoey was try'n to get away, but I kept pulling her back. As soon as my tongue touched her asshole she really went berserk.

"Oh my God! Oh my God! Ooooooh Tweek Stoooop!" I just kept going, when I blew in her ass she completely lost it.

"Shiiiiiiit! IIII'm Cummimg again Oooooooooh!" I slowly turnover while grabbing a condom off tha night stand; 4 hours, 4 condoms and about 6 orgasms later we both laid in each others arms exhausted.

"Boy you got it going on."

"So do you."

"Tweek I love you."

"Me love you more."

"I doubt that."

Tha next morning at breakfast Ciara said, "Is it me or are tha two of them glowing this morning?"

"It's just you," we both said in unison.

"Oooooooh yall had sex last night."

"No we didn't."

"It's about time you finally gave him some, shit if it was me I would've left ya ass."

"What ever and we didn't have sex."

"Maybe not physical, but yall did something."

"Cal must of put it on you last night."

"Yup he sure did and I loved every minute of it, especially when…"

"EEEEELL, please spare us tha details. Tweek you must really love my sister, yall been together for a year and still haven't did tha do yet."

"Our relationship ain't based on sex."

"So I see, but it would definitely help it. You must be getting some on tha side?"

"Nah C that ain't my style some things are worth waiting for," he said while winking at me."

"I knew it, see Cal I knew it." We finished our breakfast then headed out to do some sightseeing with tha other tourists.

"Now that's it just me and you, was it good and worth tha wait?"

"Ciara what are you talking bout?"

"Don't play, you know exactly what I'm talkin' about."

"All in my biz-ness."

"What ever, now spill it."

Sis I'm not going to front, he definitely has it going on."

"I knew you had sex cause ya face was glowing and I haven't seen you like that since Quez was alive."

"I know, but don't I deserve to be happy Sis?"

"Of course you do. I'm ready to go back to tha room so I can blow."

"And you not a weed head, yeah right. I'm not ready to leave yet."

"Me either, but I have biz-ness to attend to, not to mention we have a son."

"Well we better get downstairs so we won't miss our flight."

"Oh my God, I am so drained, I just want to go to sleep."

"We have a flight to catch, you can sleep on tha plane."

We all boarded tha plane and headed back to tha States.

CHAPTER 40

No Loyalty, No Remorse

Tha whole city was up in an uproar thanks to Jibbs, Bo, LT, and Rosco.

"Yo them niggaz on some bullshit."

"Fuck them mafuckas, I wish they would come over here wit that dumb shit."

"Cal and Tweek should be back today."

"Are you sure what you told me was accurate?"

"Yeah my cousin is Fucking that nigga Jibbs and she overheard him talking to Bo."

"Somebody is going to die behind this shit."

"Hey, he knew what tha consequences would be if it came to light."

"Yeah, but he never expected it to come to light."

"My loyalty doesn't lie wit them niggaz so Fuck 'em!

"Fuck 'em then! This is tha call we've been waiting on."

"Yo what tha biz is?"

"You tell me I just got ya message."

"Not over tha phone, where you at?"

"Leaving tha airport."

"Well, hit me after you get ya self together."

"Imma come thru in about 45 minutes."

"I'll be on tha block."

"You still holding?"

"Nah, you can bring my usual."

A hour later, me and Tweek were pulling up to Cash and PJ's block.

"Yo you two niggaz got Black as shit."

"I know."

"I know them Dominican Bitches was bad as a mafucka, wasn't they?"

"Man I don't think I seen one ugly chick tha whole trip."

"Daaamn and you niggaz took sand to tha beach?"

"So what was so important?"

"I don't know how to say it no other way, so Imma just say it. Jibbs is a shiesty nigga!"

"Tell me something we don't already know."

"How about he's tha one who had Quez killed."

"What! Nigga you playing."

I told him how we came across that info.

"So this whole time that nigga been acting like he had Zoey's back he was plotting."

"Yup, he been on some take over shit while yall were gone."

"Damn this is gonna break Zoey's heart."

"Yeah, but she needs to know."

"Why don't we just kill him and tell her then."

"Nah, she needs to know.

"What ever yall want to do, yall got our support."

"That's whats up, let me grab this work for yall so we can bounce."

We were both quite on tha ride to Zoey's house.

"I knew that mafucka was not trustworthy."

"I didn't, tha nigga had me eating, so I had a lot of respect for him and tha fact he was Ciara's cousin."

"Those be tha ones, smile in ya face, tha whole time he try'n to be tha man."

"You know we gon have to off all them niggaz."

"I know."

We dropped off tha rest of tha work then made our way to Zoey's.

"Took yall long enough."

"We had to make a few stops, you know we been gone two weeks."

"So what was so important that it couldn't wait?"

"I think you need to sit down for this."

"This must be serious."

"Very. We have information on Quez's murder."

"Oh my God!"

"You're not going to like this."

Tears started to run down her face. I walked over and sat next to her because I knew she was going to need my support once Cal told her who had Quez killed.

"Zoey there is no easy way to say this but Jibbs paid Rosco and LT to kill Quez."

"Noooooo he didn't!"

"Zoey he did." Her reaction was tha opposite of what I was expecting. So I asked her, "What are we going to do about it?"

"There's only one thing we can do about it 'Kill them all'!"

"A'ight we'll handle it."

"No I need to do this on my own."

"Zoey you know we can't let you do this by ya self, so count us in."

"I'll take care Jibbs, yall can handle tha other three."

"Fair enough."

She pulled her phone to make a call.

"Hey was you busy? A'ight stop by when you finish, I need to talk to you."

"Zoey you a'ight?"

"Yeah, I'm fine."

"A'ight we bout to get on top of that."

"Cal, Tweek, thank you and be safe."

"Always."

Me and Cal decided to take care of Rosco and LT first since they were and would be tha biggest threat.

"Yo, do you know where to find them at?"

"If I'm not mistaken they like to hang out at tha Bath House."

"Well that's where we'll catch them."

"Zoey what's wrong? I know Tweek isn't cheating?"

"No I just found out who had Quez killed."

"Who?"

"You not going to believe it."

"That means it's somebody we know."

"Jibbs."

"Bitch close ya mouth. Did I hear you correctly?"

"Yup."

"How did you find that out?"

"Cash's cousin was Fuckin' Jibbs and he must of thought she was sleep. He just didn't give a Fuck talkin like that around her whether he thought she was sleep or not."

"So now what?" I didn't have to answer that because she already knew tha answer.

"I want in."

"You don't have to be a part of this."

"I know, but I want to and what about tha rest of them?"

"Cal and Tweek are handling that." Time to put tha plan in motion.

I knew it would only be a matter of time before she called.

"Are you going to answer it?"

"Nah, if it's important she'll call back." Sure enough she called back.

"Yo!"

"Whats up Cuz?"

"Same shit different toilet."

"I wanna call a truce."

"There was never no beef on my end."

"Mines either, but while I was on vacation I had time to sit back and think on a lot of shit."

"Oh yeah?"

"Yeah."

"And?"

"And I think that I'm done wit this shit and nobody else is fit to take tha throne, except you." *Shit it's about time she see it my way, I thought to myself.*

"I need to focus more on my salon." I could tell I had his full attention so I kept it going. "Imma call a meeting wit everybody in about a day or so, so that we're all on the same page."

"All them faggots that didn't want to deal wit me ain't gon have a choice now and tha price just went up on 'em," I thought to myself.

"Did you talk to tha Connect yet?"

"Yeah, he said he's a'ight wit it so we'll sit down Friday so I can introduce yall."

"That's whats up."

"I'll hit you up a little later I'm about to go to ya moms for a little while."

"OK"

"Damn nigga you all smiles, what she say?"

"Let's just say I won't have to kill her now."

"Word, so should I put my trip to see my pops on hold?"

"Nah go head, by tha time you come back I'll be tha new King of Philly."

"Wit out killing Zoey?"

"She said she wants to get out and she wants me to take over."

"Wow! That is good news."

"Who you telling and Friday I get to meet tha Plug."

"So we don't need Roscoe or LT now?"

"They'll be history by tha time you get back."

CHAPTER 41

Revenge, Rosco, LT, and Bo Get Killed

It was a little after one in tha morning and these niggaz was still in tha Bath House. "If these niggaz don't hurry up I'm going in there guns blazing."

"You plan on doing a life bid huh?"

"Imagine that."

"Here they come now."

I went to reach for tha door but Tweek stopped me.

"What's up? There they go."

"Chill we're gonna follow 'em."

"Here put this on," I said handing him a silencer.

We stayed back so they wouldn't know that they were being followed. They ended up stopping at a Chinese store.

"Let's get 'em now."

"Cal just be patient, I got this trust me."

"Don't I always?"

"This is what we gon' do."

After telling him tha plan out we got out.

"Nigga, I'm telling you Kobe Bryant is a better player than Michael Jordan ever was."

"Nigga you stupid if you could make Jordan Kobe's age again he would shit on him."

"Yeah right."

LT and Rosco were standing in front of tha store now.

"Let's ask them."

"Excuse me."

"Yo whats up?"

"He's try'n to tell me Kobe is better than Jordan."

"He is."

"In ya Fuckin dreams."

"I think Jordan is better."

"Told you nigga."

"Nah, Kobe is better."

"That's what I say."

"Yall not from around here, are yall?"

"Why?"

"Cause these young boys be on some dumb shit."

"Let me get my heat out tha car before we get caught slippin."

"To late," I said pulling out my Desert Eagle (semi-automatic handgun).

"Please don't run," Cal said wit his 45 pointed at LT's face.

"Look I don't have no money on me, but a couple hundred."

"Mafucka I don't want ya money."

"Well, what do you want then?"

"Ya life!"

PIT! PIT! PIT!

3 shots to his face sent him to his maker. Rosco tried to run, but Cal unloaded his whole clip in his back. Just to make sure he was dead I turned him over and put one in his dome. We left just as quietly as we

came headed to Bo's house.

"Looks like we came right on time."

"It's 2:30 in tha morning, where this nigga headed?"

"I don't know, but we bout to find out come on!"

"Damn nigga, where you headed?"

"Oh shit, you niggaz scared tha shit out of me."

"You must be doing something you ain't got no biz-ness doing."

"Nah, I'm bout to visit my pops for a few days."

"Oh."

"What yall doing over this side of town?"

"My young jawn live down tha street."

"So you tired of Zoey already?"

"Nah, but you know a nigga always gotta have side piece too."

"True dat."

"Well, you be easy, we'll see you when you get back."

"A'ight."

As soon as he turned his back 'PIT, PIT' two shots to his head.

"Help me put him in tha trunk."

"We gon just leave him in tha trunk?"

"Nah, I got a better ideal, follow me."

Twenty minutes later we were pulling up to this junk yard.

"What are we doing here Tweek?"

"My cousin owns this place."

"That still doesn't answer my question."

He didn't answer me, he just unlocked tha gate then drove thru. I got out of tha car to assist him.

"I got it, just stay right here."

I stood back and watched as he got in tha crane then lifted tha car up, sitting it under tha crusher. Once tha car was compacted to tha size of a shopping cart, Tweek put it in wit tha other compacted cars.

"Cal turn that hose on so I can clean this blood up."

CHAPTER 42

Ms. Wilma Reveals Disturbing News

Fifteen minutes later we were on our way back to tha block. We pulled up, tha block was jumping as usual.

"Cal can speak to you for a minute please?"

"Sure Ms. Wilma what's up?"

"I have some disturbing news."

"Do I need to sit down for this Ms. Wilma?"

"You might want to because you're not gonna like what I have to tell you."

"Who came up short?"

"Nobody."

"Then what has you so upset?"

"Remember when we got robbed a few months back?"

"How could I forget, I took tha lost remember."

"Well, my niece hangs wit this girl and tha girl was wearing tha necklace my niece brought me."

"Is that tha necklace you said they took?"

"Yes, so anyway she asked her where she got it and she said her man who just happens to be none other than ya boy Box."

"What!"

"You heard me, Box."

"But he got shot."

"That was just to make it look good."

"Now it's all starting to make sense."

"What's that?"

"His hostility that night, Ms. Wilma he was on some bullshit, but now I know why."

Before I left I asked Ms. Wilma if KC or Glass were involved, but she didn't know.

"Don't worry I won't say anything," I smiled and walked out.

"Tweek, Ms. Wilma just told me that Box was tha one who hit tha house."

"I had a feeling he had something to do wit it."

"Why didn't you say something?"

"I wasn't 100 percent and I bet tha two mask men were KC and Glass," we said in unison.

"I know we gon' handle it."

"Witout a doubt."

My phone started to ring...

"Hello." Time to come home was all she said then hung up

"That was tha Mrs., I'll hit you in tha AM."

I pulled up to my house because I figured Zoey wanted to be alone, but I was wrong, she was laying on my couch when I walked in.

"I figured you would come home instead of my house."

"I didn't think you wanted to be bothered after finding out Jibbs had Quez killed."

"He's not going to be around too much longer, I have a meeting set up tha day after tomorrow."

"Well Roscoe, LT, and Bo all have been sent to tha boneyard courtesy of me."

"Cal did not help?"

"Yeah, he hit Rosco, but truth be told, I would have rather took care of it myself."

"Why is that?"

"It was personal to me, they hurt you so I wanted to hurt them. Tha crazy thing is, if they never killed Quez, me and you wouldn't be together today and I wouldn't have mind knowing you on a friend level." She didn't respond wit words only her tongue going into my mouth.

"Tweek don't take this tha wrong way, but I do wish Quez was still alive and yes I do still miss him."

"How could I take that tha wrong way, you two were together for almost all of your lives, I would actually be offended if you didn't still feel that way about him."

"Don't get me wrong I don't regret meeting you and for tha last 13 months I've been nothing but happy wit you as my mate. Not to mention, I fell head over heels in love wit you."

"Zoey I knew that we were either going to be lovers or really good friends." "Oh really," she said.

"Yeah I even told Cal so. And I didn't really trust Jibbs for some reason, but Cal told me he was good peoples. And despite my instincts and tha strength of Cal I decided to Fuck wit him and look if he would do that to his own blood then what would he do to me Now, I've always been tha type of nigga that if I seen somebody getting money, I hustled harder to get more money. Well, Jibbs thought by killing Quez he would be in control." We talked until we fell asleep in each others arms.

CHAPTER 43

Kill 3 Birds wit One Stone

Tha next morning Cal called bright and early.

"Get ya sleepy ass up, nigga we got a full day on our hands."

"Man I been up, I'm eating my breakfast."

"A'ight I'm on my way."

"Didn't I say I was eating breakfast."

"You should be done by tha time I get there."

"I'll meet you on tha block in 45 minutes."

"Forty five minutes? Damn nigga what kind of breakfast you eating? Ha! Ha! Ha!"

"Oh shit right, right I got you, just hurry up and make sure you brush your teeth."

I finished my breakfast, jumped in tha shower, then bounced.

"I thought I was going to have to put out a APB."

"Now you got jokes."

"Nah but on some serious shit, Box has to be laid to rest, I'm not sure if KC and Glass were in on it, but if I had to guess I would say they were. I'm saying that to say tha choice is yours whether they live or die."

"I think you already know tha answer to that."

"Well let's get this day started."

I was hurt that Box, my childhood friend would betray me like this after all that I have done for him.

"Zoey told me to let you know there's a meeting tomorrow night at tha Warehouse at 9 o'clock.

"We can kill 3 birds wit one stone."

"How?"

"I know where they eat breakfast every morning."

"Nigga you always on ya shit."

"I gotta be in this game."

"You right about that, I always knew you was a smart young boy."

"Cal I may be young in age, but I'm old when it comes to these streets. I been in these streets since tha age of 9, I've seen and been through it all."

"I can tell by tha way you took care of that situation last wit those niggaz night."

"There they go pulling in now."

"Yup 9 o'clock on tha dot just like you said."

"Wait here while I do what I have to do, if somebody comes out just blow tha horn."

"No problem." I sat in tha car and watched as Tweek rolled under tha car to hook up tha tracking device so I thought.

"Come on."

"Where we going?"

"Did you eat breakfast yet?"

"No, but you did," I said laughing Ha! Ha! Ha!

"Let's grab a bite to eat."

As soon as we walked in Box, KC, and Glass were staring at us.

"Dining in or out?" tha waitress asked?

"To go."

After we placed our order I walked over to their table.

"Glass, KC what's up I haven't seen yall in a minute," I said not acknowledging Box which I knew had him in his bag.

"We been on some money shit down Delaware."

I knew they were lying so I said, "Oh yeah what part? I've got people down there." Before they could answer Cal walked up.

"What's tha deal yall?"

"Same shit," Box said wit an obvious attitude.

"I come in peace, no need for that," Cal said wit a smile.

"Well yall be easy, it was good seeing yall," I said referring to KC and Glass.

"You too nigga."

"Look at those two mafuckas," Box said ice grilling tha back of their heads.

"I can't wait to get them this time around Imma take everything. Let's pay tha tab and get outta here before I catch a homicide." We paid for our food and headed out tha same time as they were coming out.

"Aye Tweek."

"Yo."

"You still got tha same number?"

"Yeah, it ain't change."

"A'ight Imma hit you up, maybe we can do some biz-ness. We finally got our money up like you said.

"I doubt that," I said to myself.

But instead I said, "Just hit me up and ain't no hard feelings about that money."

Nobody said shit, they just looked at each other. At that moment I new what I was about to do was right.

"Tweek, what was that about?"

"I just wanted to see if they broke into my moms crib."

"I guess you got ya answer."

"Sure did."

"Well, we know where to find them since you put that tracking device on their car."

"What tracking device?"

"Tha one you put under their car."

"Oh you mean this?" As soon as they pulled out tha parking lot I hit tha switch, wit in seconds...BOOM! Tha whole car blew up.

"Oh shit!"

I didn't say shit, I just slowly pulled off. Right then and there I knew Tweek was definitely about his biz-ness by any means necessary.

"I guess that's what you meant when you said kill 3 birds wit one stone?" He still didn't say nothing but smiled.

For tha remainder of tha day we hit tha block and listened to all tha different rumors about what happened to Glass, KC, and Box. This one girl said she was right there when tha mob pulled up and threw a grenade in tha car. They also said tha car caught on fire while they were driving. Tha craziest one was that two Russians pulled up on tha side of them on a motorcycle and shot tha gas tank. "Cal I don't feel bad for them."

"Me either, just Box's daughter she really loved him. I had no ideal that he had a Trust Fund set up for her just in case something like this happened."

CHAPTER 44

Betrayal and Deceit a Deadly Combination

That night I sat back and thought about tha last 48 hours of my life.

"Baby are you a'ight? What's wrong?"

"Nothin just thinking about how you could be tha best of friends wit somebody and think you know them but you really don't!"

"Yeah, I feel tha same way about family."

"Baby betrayal and deceit is a deadly combination."

"I would never betray somebody that I have love for."

"Everybody ain't you, money changes people."

"That's why I have no remorse for killing them niggaz, none of them, and I would do it again if it came down to it to protect myself or tha people I love!"

"Tweek you're too good to be true and as crazy as it may sound, I think Quez sent you to me."

"Cal are you OK? "

"Yeah just thinking about how lucky I am to have you and Calry in my life."

"No we're tha lucky ones."

"Ciara when I had nothing you never complained, you just did what needed to be done to make sure we stayed afloat."

"No Cal, I did what any real woman would have done in that situation, stand by her man. Don't get me wrong I like tha finer things in life, but I'm not materialistic."

"I'll be home late tonight, me and Tweek have a whole lot to do today."

"I'm cooking ya favorite tonight, just in case you want to take a little break and come eat wit your family."

"I can take a hint, I'll be home to eat wit yall."

From doing so much running around I had lost track of time.

"Cal I don't know about you but I'm hungry as shit."

"Me too, oh shit!"

"What?"

"I promised Ciara I would come home to eat wit her and Calry."

"You better get there, I'll meet you at tha Warehouse at 9."

"You don't wanna join us?"

"Nah, go eat wit ya family."

"Nigga you are family."

"Me and Zoey already got dinner."

"So I guess you'll be coming wit her to tha meeting then?"

"Yeah, her and Zell."

"A'ight, well I'll see you then."

After dinner we picked Zell up then made our way to tha meeting spot. By tha time we got there everybody was already there including tha Guest of Honor Jibbs.

When we walked in Cal said, "I was beginning to think yall wasn't coming."

"Let's get started," Jibbs said all smiles.

"Well I know yall wondering why I called this meeting."

"Yeah and why is this mafucka here?" PJ questioned.

"Nigga you better stay in ya lane if you know what's best for you."

PJ stood up. "Nigga ain't no guns in here," he said challenging Jibbs.

"Won't be none of that in here."

"As you all know a little over a year ago Quez was killed. Tha police thought it was a drunk driver, but they later called it a murder."

Everybody looked shocked except Jibbs.

"Well anyway, I took over his biz-ness and we have all made a lot of money since."

"I know I have!" somebody yelled out.

"I think it's time for me to hand tha reigns over so I could put more time into my salon. Therefore Jibbs will be taking over for me."

"Hell no! Fuck that! I'm talkin my biz-ness elsewhere!"

"Listen you mafuckas don't have to do biz-ness wit me, but I guarantee it would be hard for you to eat."

"That's exactly why I don't want to deal wit him, he's too cocky."

"Jibbs if that's tha approach you're taking then I don't think this will work."

"Zoey you've been pampering these niggaz too damn long."

"Loyalty Jibbs Loyalty, L-O-Y-A-L-T-Y," I said spelling it out just to make sure he understood.

"So what are you saying Zoey?"

"They have loyalty and I trust them."

"You can trust me too!"

"Can I trust you Jibbs?"

"Where is this coming from Zoey?"

"I never thought that you of all people would betray me like taking tha one thing that meant tha world to me!"

"What are you talking about?"

"Mafucka do not play dumb wit me," she said pulling out her 45.

"Whoa, Whoa!"

"I know that you, Bo, LT, and Rosco killed Quez and please don't try to deny it."

Zoey had tears coming down her face.

"These are tears for ya mom because it's going to break her heart when you're gone. Do you have anything to say?"

"Bo knows about this meeting so if you kill me he will kill you."

"I doubt that, he's already dead and you already know about tha other two. All you had to do was ask Quez and he would have made sure you ate."

"Fuck that nigga and Fuck you too Bitch!"

BOOM! BOOM!

Tha first two shots hit him center forehead killing him instantly. And just to get tha pain out, she stood over him and dumped tha rest of her clip into his lifeless body wit no remorse.

"Let this be a lesson to anybody that thinks he can get away wit anything."

"So you're not stepping down?"

"Oh I am stepping down and these two will be running things from this day forward."

Me and Tweek looked at one another, this was tha first we heard about this. Once tha meeting was over we took Jibbs body somewhere so that it could easily be found. Leave it up to Tweek to make it look like a drug deal gone bad or should I say turned robbery.

Tha story on tha front page read:

DRUG DEAL TURNED ROBBERY A TALE OF BETRAYAL & DECEIT!

We got tha call from Mya; Zoey didn't show any emotion.

"I'll be by tha house in a little while."

"Baby I know its going to be a little hard, but try and show some emotion."

"I will once I see my aunt going through it."

We spent tha next few days helping my aunt prepare for tha funeral. Tha day of tha funeral I chose to ride wit Zell and Tweek instead of tha Limo wit tha family. Truth be told, I didn't even really want to go to tha funeral, but outta respect for my family I did. They always say keep ya friends and enemies close, but family even closer.

Over tha next year my salon had really made a name for itself and we even had a few celebrities coming in to get hooked up. Cal and Tweek had ventured out of state wit their biz-ness. Zell moved to New York wit Spence after their wedding. Oh yeah before I forget, me and Tweek are expecting a son in 2 months. Always remember, where there is BETRAYAL, DECEIT is not far behind.

ABOUT THE AUTHOR

My name is Jerz Toston and I started writing books while I was incarcerated as a means to pass time, but soon realized that I not only had a gift for writing but also a passion for it. So I continued to perfect my craft during my 60 months.

This hasn't been an easy journey, but I wouldn't change a thing about it. Never let anyone tell you that you can't. Jus prove em wrong. This is jus tha 1st of many and its only gonna get better.

www.ingramcontent.com/pod-product-compliance
Lightning Source LLC
Chambersburg PA
CBHW070443120726
47910CB00003B/910